HE WAS A LIAR

DANIEL HURST

www.danielhurstbooks.com

This is a work of fiction. Names, characters, businesses, places, events, locales, and incidents are either the products of the author's imagination or used in a fictitious manner. Any resemblance to actual persons, living or dead, or actual events is entirely coincidental.

PROLOGUE

Honesty is important in any relationship. It's the foundation on which everything else is built. That is why I have always strived to be honest with everybody in my life.

Family members. Friends. Partners.

Especially partners.

In return, I always expected I would get that same kind of honesty back. I assumed I would. But I guess I was being naïve. Not everybody is as honest as me. People lie. It's just a part of life, and it's just another problem to be dealt with, like bad traffic or finding out that you left your purse at home just as you get to the shops. But there are different kinds of lies. There are the white lies, the kind that aren't truthful but aren't exactly devastating, like somebody saying that your hair looks nice even if it doesn't. And then there are the bigger lies, like telling somebody something so open and raw that it can't be anything but honest, except it is a lie, and it has the power to tear out your heart when you unravel it.

I have been told all sorts of lies in my time, from the innocent to the downright dirty. But none of them could compare to the lie I was told by my late partner, Paul. He told me the one thing that every person in a relationship wants to hear.

He told me that I was the only one for him.

That was a lie, and I'm still struggling to come to terms with it today. Paul was not the man I thought he was. He was a liar, and it's just a shame I only found out about it after his death.

I wish I'd found out before he died.

That way, I could have killed him myself.

1

JUST BEFORE PAUL DIED

Time seems to have almost come to a standstill, and the reason for that is the day of the week. It's Sunday, and it's the middle of the morning. For me, my partner and millions of other people around the country right now, that means no work to go to and no boring chores to be done. Instead, all we have to do is stay under the duvet and do as little as possible for as long as possible.

Needless to say, this is my favourite time of the week.

'Don't move, Sarah. You have something on your eyelash.'

I freeze as Paul stares intently into my eyes before I close them to allow him to remove whatever it is that he has spotted. With my eyes shut, I feel his fingers gently wiping my eyelids before he tells me that it is okay to open them again.

'What was it?' I ask him, looking at his fingers that are still close to my face.

'A piece of fluff,' he replies, showing me the tiny white thing on the end of one of his fingers before bringing it up to his mouth and gently blowing it away across the bed.

'My hero,' I say sarcastically as I rub my eyes just to make sure there isn't any more fluff around them, or sleepy dust, or anything that might make the man lying in this bed next to me wonder why he is with me and not with a more attractive woman that he could surely find if he wanted to look. But I know that he doesn't want to look for another woman because he loves me, and he's told me that far too many times to count since we began dating ten years ago.

A decade is a long time by anybody's standards, but I mean it when I say that the period has passed in what feels like the blink of an eye. Being with Paul has been an absolute pleasure, and it's hard to remember what my life was like before he was in it. I had only been twenty-six and still very much in the midst of my youth when I made eye contact with the handsome man at the other end of the busy bar that I was enjoying a Saturday night in. At the time, I'd been out with friends expecting nothing more than a good laugh, some drinking and dancing and a bit of a sore head the next morning. But what I ended up getting was something slightly more fruitful than that.

I got myself a boyfriend.

Paul and I got chatting that night, we swapped numbers at the end of it, and then we met up shortly afterwards for our very first date. It was to be the beginning of a romance that has lasted all the way to the present day, where I'm much older and much wiser, or at least that's what I like to think anyway. But really, I feel like I am still the same person I was when I met Paul all those years ago, and I think that is a testament to him as a boyfriend. He has never tried to change me or make me do anything I didn't want to do just for the sake of our relationship. He encourages me to go out just as much with my friends as I did before we met, and he supports me in my career where I have worked as a production assistant at the same local television studio ever since I graduated from university. He compliments me on my appearance, no matter whether it is a good hair day or a bad one, and he never tries to dissuade me from having that last slice of pizza or garlic bread, even if a couple of inches have crept onto my waistline in the time we have been together.

I suppose he is just being a good boyfriend in being that way, but I know from experience that not all men are like him. I've had a few exes who weren't shy in telling me what to do or, rather, what not to do, and I know my friends have had their fair share of problematic relationships too. That's why I'm so lucky with Paul. He doesn't care about anything other than what makes me happy every day, whether that's getting dressed up for a night on the town or spending all day lounging on the sofa in my baggy pyjamas without a hint of makeup on my face.

He loves me just as I am.

And the feeling is mutual.

Paul is the kind of guy every parent would want their daughter to bring home one day. He is polite and witty, with enough of a professional side to hold down a stable job but also enough of a mischievous side to be good fun at social events. He is kind, caring and driven, but also relaxed enough to go with the flow and take life as it comes. He is a good guy, and you would only have to ask his family, friends and work colleagues to back that up.

Oh, and did I mention that he is gorgeous?

Because he is.

All in all, it would appear that I have snared myself a good man in a world that isn't as full of them as people might like to think. That's why I've been with him for ten years, and it's also why I'm hoping to be with him for the next fifty. There's no reason to think that our relationship won't go on and on and stand the test of time, and I'm sure we will be fine whatever happens. But there is one more thing that could make things even more perfect between us.

He could propose to me.

I estimate that it would only take me around 1.2 seconds to say yes.

Don't get me wrong, I'm not dreaming of a white wedding every day, and I'm certainly not putting my partner under any kind of pressure to buy me a ring and pop the question, but I would be lying if I said I didn't want it to happen sometime soon. I am in my mid-thirties now, and that's a time when things really need to be happening in a woman's life if that woman dreams of one day having children with a man she loves. I don't think being married would make my relationship with Paul any stronger than it already is, but it would be nice to showcase our love in front of our family and friends, all of whom I just know are desperate to see us tie the knot.

Some of my friends do think it is a little strange that Paul hasn't proposed yet, considering how long we have been together, and many of them are married now even though they met their partners years after I met

Paul. My sister, Ellen, is always asking me when I am going to get hitched and start popping out babies like she has, although to be fair to her, she is honest with her reasoning and only wants me to be married with kids because then I'll be 'as miserable as she is'. She's only joking, of course, and she loves her husband and two daughters, but it's just her way of trying to make me see that perhaps I need to be a little more forceful with Paul when it comes to our future plans. But I don't want to put him under any pressure, and I'm certainly not going to sit him down and have a serious talk to establish a timeline of when we can do all the things that most of the other people our age are already doing. Just like we did when we first met, we're taking things one day at a time. It's worked for us this far, and I have no reason to suspect it will ever stop working for us in the future.

'I'm starving. Shall we get a takeaway?' Paul suddenly says before reaching for his mobile phone on the bedside table.

'I think it might be a little too early for a takeaway,' I say with a smile before checking the time on my own phone and confirming that it is.

'Is pizza before noon considered unhealthy?'

'I'm pretty sure even the guy making the pizza for you would be disgusted at your behaviour.'

Paul laughs and drops his phone back onto the table, presumably giving up on his silly idea of trying to find somebody who could deliver him some junk food at ten-thirty in the morning. But it seems he won't be put off from his dodgy diet by the time of day.

‘How about some snacks then? I could go to the corner shop and get us a few things. We could chill out with a few bags of crisps and a movie until we reach a more acceptable time to order pizza.’

‘Hmmm, I like the sound of that. What flavour of crisps are you thinking?’

‘I’m thinking of getting a bag of every flavour. And a bar of chocolate or two while I’m at it.’

Paul gives me that cheeky smile of his, and I beam right back at him because this is just one of the many things that I love about this man. Some guys might have their partners out of bed early on a Sunday morning to go for a run or at least have some kind of a healthy breakfast. But my boyfriend knows that I’m not interested in anything like that today. All I want to do is chill out with him and enjoy some tasty food without any of the guilt that is sometimes associated with it. Thank God too, because I’m a useless runner, and I’ve never been a fan of avocado or granola to start my day.

Paul peels back the duvet, revealing his bare torso and his skimpy pair of boxer shorts before getting out of bed and wandering around the room, scooping up his various items of clothing from the floor. I take a moment to watch him as he works, ogling his nice body that never seems to show any of the signs of all the fatty food and drink he likes to put down his throat at the weekends. I wish I had a metabolism like his, but I don’t, and that’s why I’m keeping the duvet on top of myself, so that my love handles can stay covered up now that we’re in broad daylight. Paul doesn’t care if I’m a little jigglier around the edges now than when I met him, but I sometimes do, and right now, I'll keep myself hidden.

I'll stay like this until he brings me back my snacks.

'Do you want me to come with you?' I ask him as he pulls his t-shirt over his head, but he'll already know by my tone of voice that I'm not really serious about getting up and joining him out there on the chilly streets.

'No, it's fine. You stay here and find us a movie to watch when I get back,' he replies, and I smile at him because that sounds like a good plan to me.

I grab the remote control from my bedside table and turn the television on as Paul finishes getting ready, and it's not long until he comes over to give me a kiss and tell me that he'll be back soon.

'I love you,' I say to him as he heads for the door and for a second, I almost think that he isn't going to say it back, which would be very unlike him. But then he pauses just before he walks out of the room and looks back to where I am lazily lying in the warm bed, and he flashes me that dazzling smile of his again.

'I love you too,' he says with warmth and meaning.

And then he leaves me.

2

I can feel my stomach rumbling slightly as I lie on my mattress with my head on a pillow and my eyes on the television screen across the room. I'm watching the news, but my mind is on all the tasty treats that Paul will be bringing back for me soon. The corner shop is only a ten-minute walk away, so I shouldn't have to wait too long for him to return with a bag of snacks in his hand and a big grin on his handsome face. But until I see him walk back into this bedroom, I will pass the time by watching TV.

Sadly, while Sunday mornings are almost unbeatable, Sunday morning television is not. It always seems to be a choice between a few 'celebrities' on a cooking show or a bunch of dreary old men on a politics panel, and I've never been much of a chef or a supporter of any kind of political party, so I've skipped through those channels. In the end, I've settled on watching the national news for lack of a better option, and even though there will be politics discussed here, I'm sure that it will be interspersed with a few more interesting stories. And at least this way I don't have to watch some Z-List celebrity talking about her next book while cooking (and burning) an omelette.

So far, the news today has covered a violent protest in Bolivia and the uncovering of a sexual abuse scandal at a large media company in Berlin, but it's sometimes hard to really feel the impact of a story that is taking place miles away from where I am right now. But all that changes when the next item comes on the agenda because this is very much a story that happened closer to home.

The first thing I see on screen is the same photo that I've seen countless times over the last year before I hear the reporter say the name that I and everybody else in Britain are all too familiar with now. It's Charlotte Graham, and she is the eighteen-year-old student who went missing last September and has never been seen since.

This is a story that has dominated the headlines from the time it broke, and there have been all sorts of theories about what has happened to Charlotte, although none of them can ever be certified as the truth until either she comes home or her body is found, neither of which have happened yet. I turn the volume up a little bit when I hear the reporter start talking about her because I wonder if there has been some kind of breakthrough in the case, but then I learn that it's just another appeal for information ahead of the twelve-month anniversary of her disappearance next week. I keep watching as I see her parents appear on screen, their familiar faces showing their familiar distress as they talk about their daughter and how desperate they are to know the truth. But like the millions of other people around the country who want to know the truth too, the wait goes on, and maybe it will never end.

As the news reporter moves onto another topic and I turn the volume down again, I am struck by a troubling thought that I have had more than once since the whole sorry situation with Charlotte entered the public consciousness. It's the thought that tells me that maybe having a child of my own is not worth all the stress and worry that goes into being a mother. I've seen via Charlotte's parents what it is like to lose a child and be powerless to get them back, and I'm not sure I could handle that level of trauma and fear. Those poor people are going through hell right now while here I am lazing around in bed with my only worry being what kind of crisps I am going to be eating in a few moments' time. There's no denying that I have a very carefree existence, but all that would change if Paul and I were to have a baby together. I'd go from having nothing to worry about to having everything to worry about and while I'm sure there is more good than bad when one becomes a parent, try telling that to Charlotte's parents now. They'll never get over what has happened to their daughter, even though they don't even know what has happened, and that thought is a terrifying one. I don't think I'm ready for having a little life to look after, and even if I do somehow make it through eighteen years of raising them to be an adult, how do I know something horrible isn't going to happen to them once they are out of my care? There are dangerous people in the world, and I'm guessing Charlotte fell foul of one of them. But what if that happened to my child? How could I go on, having lost somebody who I cared about so much?

My eyes continue to watch the footage on the TV screen, but I'm not really processing the images of the angry mob in South Africa. Instead, I'm thinking about how scary it would be to lose someone who I loved. Of course, I have always had family members and friends who I love, but it would be a deeper level of pain if I lost a child, just like I feel it would be a deeper level of pain if I lost Paul. The ten years I've had with him have been the best years of my life, and there has barely been a day go by when we haven't seen each other. But if there was a rare occasion when we were apart in all that time then we would always make sure to speak over the phone, telling the other one about our day and letting them know how much we missed them and couldn't wait to be reunited again. I dread to think what would happen to me if anything happened to Paul. He has been my rock since my mid-twenties, and I hope he will be the same thing until I reach my mid-nineties. There's no denying that we will have to part one day, and there's no saying which of us will go first, but I just hope it doesn't happen until we are old and grey and have a lifetime of memories to look back on. Who knows, though? Life is unpredictable, and that's supposed to be what makes it fun.

The problem is, it also makes it terrifying.

I continue to watch the news bulletin, but my eyes start to feel a little heavy as the minutes go by, and eventually, I stop watching the TV altogether as my eyelids close and I relax in the darkness that exists just before sleep. I'm not tired, or at least I don't think that I am, but I guess I must be because even though I can still hear the TV, I don't reopen my eyes to look at it. I just keep them shut, as if I am tempting myself to fall asleep even though I know Paul will be back any second now, and he will have food to give me when he gets here. But it does feel good to just rest, and this is what lazy

Sunday mornings are for after all, so I keep resting until the inevitable happens, and I fall asleep.

My body is still and silent while my mind races behind my closed eyes, the beginning of a dream starting to take shape as I go from watching artificial entertainment in the real world to experiencing deeply personal entertainment in my slumber. For some reason, I'm in a studio, and the lights are bright and the cameras are pointing in my direction. It feels a little overwhelming, but then the man beside me tells me to take my time and not to worry because he will be there with me every step of the way. I have no idea what he is talking about until I look down and see the empty bowl in front of me. Then the man slides a packet of eggs across the worktop and tells me to take out four of them.

What's happening? Am I making a cake? No, apparently, I'm making bread, and there are thousands of people watching me do it in the hopes that they will soon know how to make this same thing too. I'm on a cookery show, and that means that I am definitely dreaming. But this isn't a nightmare, even if I am some kind of Z-list celeb in this world, so that's why I don't wake up and go back to my real life. Instead, I just keep sleeping and just keep dreaming, and that's why it isn't long until I am standing proudly in front of a freshly baked loaf of bread that the host of this TV show is complimenting me on.

I guess I'm not so bad in the kitchen after all, and maybe these cookery shows aren't so bad either. But of course, this is not real life. I'm asleep, and things are easy in this world or certainly much easier than in the real world anyway, where I couldn't make bread to save my life. But dreams can't last forever, and this one will be no different. Pretty soon, I am going to wake up again, and when I do, things will never be the same again.

3

The television is still on when I wake up, but the news has finished. I stare at the screen for a couple of seconds as I slowly come out of my slumber and watch as a famous person I have heard of interviews a famous person who I haven't. But once I'm awake, it doesn't take me long to look around the bedroom and see that Paul still isn't back yet.

I have no idea how long I was out for, so I grab my phone to check the time, and when I do, I'm shocked. It's past noon, meaning Sunday morning is over, and we're now into the afternoon, which means it definitely isn't acceptable to still be lounging in bed. I was asleep for almost two hours. I guess I must have needed it. But all I need now is my partner.

'Paul?' I call out from my position on the bed, but there is no response.

I assume he is in the house somewhere and decided to leave me to get some rest when he came back from the shops and found me asleep. But I feel a little guilty for dozing off, so I decide to get up, not wanting to leave him stuck on his own all day while I nap. We're supposed to be spending the day together, and besides, I'm really hungry now, and I need to find out if there are snacks left over from his trip or if I slept through the consumption of them.

Treading across the bedroom carpet in my bare feet, I think about going into the hallway in just my nightie but decided to grab my dressing gown at the last second because it's not as warm out of bed as it was in it. I tie the knot in my dressing gown around my waist before opening the bedroom door and peering out for any sign of my partner.

'Paul?' I try again, figuring he'll be able to hear me now that the door is open. But there is still no response, and now I'm intrigued as to where he could be and what he could be up to. I can't hear the TV on downstairs, nor can I hear the radio from the kitchen, so whatever he is doing, he's being very quiet.

After finding the bathroom empty too, I head down the stairs, calling out Paul's name a couple more times as I go, but the continued lack of any kind of response has me coming to the conclusion that he must be out in the garden. It's not exactly warm out there, but it's not raining either, so maybe he fancied taking his snacks outside and enjoying the fresh air.

Heading through more empty rooms without any joy, I reach the kitchen and head straight for the back door, not even bothering to glance through the window that overlooks the back garden because he has to be out here now. But then I open the door and find out the truth.

He's still nowhere to be seen.

'Where are you?' I mutter to myself, annoyed at myself for falling asleep earlier but now starting to get annoyed at my struggle to locate my partner. If he's playing hide and seek then he's doing a good job of it because I've got no idea where he could be.

Walking back through the house, I look around for any signs that would tell me that he came back from the shops. His coat. Shoes. Keys. But I can't see any of them. There's no coat hanging on the bannister, no shoes by the front door and no set of keys on the kitchen counter where he always leaves them. It's as if he hasn't come back, but it's been two hours, and he was only going around the corner.

He has to be back, doesn't he?

I go over to the curtains that are still closed in front of the living room window and pull them open but not because I want our neighbours to know that the people in this house have finally got up in the afternoon. It's because I'm checking to see if Paul is out at the front, perhaps talking to a neighbour or maybe washing the car. But he's not out there, although the car is, which still doesn't help much because he was walking to the shops, not driving.

Now I'm really puzzled, and the only thing left to do is give him a call.

I left my phone on my bedside table, so I hurry back up the stairs and grab it as quickly as I can, starting to get a little concerned about things now. I'm still sure that everything is fine, but I'll only really know that when I either see my partner or hear from him, so I call his number and put my phone to my ear.

One ring. Two rings. Three. Four. Five.

And then it goes to his voicemail.

I hang up before leaving a message, more because I'm surprised not to get through to him than for any other reason, but now I am worried. Paul wouldn't just disappear on me, even if he had come back from the shops and found me asleep. If he was going somewhere else then he would have sent me a text or left me a note.

He wouldn't just go somewhere without telling me. I've got ten years of experience with him to know that.

So what is going on?

I try his number again, but resort to sending him a text message when he still doesn't pick up. But I realise that I'm not going to get many answers if I just wait around here, so I decide to take a walk to the corner shop myself because as far as I know, that was the last place he was going to.

I'm not expecting to find him at the shop because I seriously doubt he has been hanging around there for two hours, but I have to do something, so I quickly get dressed and then head for the front door.

There's a cold breeze blowing as I lock the door and walk up the driveway, passing the car before reaching the pavement and looking both ways down the street. I'm hoping to see him coming towards me with a couple of shopping bags in hand and a story to tell me about how he bumped into an old friend or perhaps got caught up in some kind of drama on the high street and got delayed. I don't care what it is as long as I can see him coming home. But the street is empty. Paul is not here, which means I still don't know what's happened to him, and that's why I have no choice but to start walking in the direction of the corner shop.

I curse myself for falling asleep as I go, feeling like this mystery wouldn't have happened if I had stayed awake. Even if Paul had failed to come back when I was awake then I would have realised something was wrong after half an hour and given him a call then instead of leaving it so long now. I tell myself that everything is going to be okay, but I also know it's pretty pointless because I won't know that until I find him.

I'm hurrying down the street with my eyes focused ahead of me in case Paul does suddenly appear. But the only people I see are unrecognisable pedestrians who are in a hurry like I am, although surely their haste is just down to the cold wind and not because they are worried about their partner's safety.

It doesn't take me long to reach the end of the street, and I make a left turn at the end of it, knowing that I'm now halfway to the corner shop that Paul had ventured to. There's still no sign of him here, and I quicken my pace again as my heart hammers in my chest, and my breathing becomes heavier. I'm trying to stay calm, but I'm seriously beginning to think that something bad has happened. It has to have done because this is so out of character for my boyfriend. But right now, I would be happy to find out he had behaved out of character. Maybe he decided against going to the shop and went to the pub instead. Perhaps he got a call from a friend about going to a football match, and he's now standing on a terrace somewhere with a beer in his hand rather than back home with me. It would be annoying if he had done anything like that, never mind disrespectful, but at least it would mean that he was okay.

It's surprisingly quiet as I reach the end of the second street and prepare to turn the final corner that will give me a view of the corner shop. I know that it's Sunday, and the roads are usually less busy then because most people are at home, but there has been a surprising lack of vehicles passing me by since I left the house. The roads are empty, and I've never known it to be this quiet since I moved here, which was just before I met Paul. I bought my house back when I was single, figuring I wasn't going to wait to meet my Prince Charming before I got on the property ladder and stopped throwing money away on rent. The fact I ended up meeting a guy and falling in love so soon after I got the keys to my own place was a little annoying because it would have been better if I could have gone halves with my boyfriend on a house, but in the end, it didn't matter. I asked Paul to move in with me once we had got close, and he has been paying his share of the mortgage ever since. We have talked about moving somewhere a little bigger one day, but he's never been in a rush, and I'm not either. I like it around here. It's quiet.

But never this quiet.

I reach the end of the street and turn the corner, completely unaware that in doing so, I am enjoying the last second of my life before my world comes crashing down. Once I survey the scene in front of me then things will never be the same again.

I see the corner shop.

I see the ambulances parked in front of it.

I see the police cars blocking the road in both directions.

I see shell-shocked witnesses mixed in with nosy passers-by standing on the pavements and gawking.

And I see a body bag in the middle of the road, resting on the concrete.

Somehow, in that moment, I know who is inside it.

4

The policewoman with the big brown eyes and the thin nose has been talking to me for a while now, but I'm still struggling to comprehend what she has been telling me. It's as if my brain is refusing to process her words in favour of waiting for somebody else to come along and offer it better ones. But the problem is that I don't think anybody else is going to do that. I'm stuck with this woman and the words she is saying to me, no matter how scary and shocking they are.

I remember feeling stressed as I left my house and walked along the street in the direction of the corner, but in hindsight, that time was a happy one. It was certainly much happier than the time I'm going through right now, having walked around that corner and seen the dramatic scene before me.

It hadn't taken me long to assess the situation outside the corner shop and realise that somebody had been run over by a car. The sight of so many emergency service vehicles in one place was always going to be a bit of a giveaway before even getting to the body bag on the ground. But it was also the sight of the car that had come to a stop on the road at a strange angle not far from where the bag was lying that told me this had been a tragic accident. The car looked like it had just been abandoned rather than parked, and it was presumably the vehicle that had been involved in this accident. It didn't take much brainpower to work out that the crying man with his hands on his head had been the driver, and the police officers standing around him were obviously there to make sure he didn't try and flee the scene without facing the consequences of what he had done. But he wasn't going anywhere. He had been too distressed to even think about that. He had just stayed still and kept staring at the bag.

He didn't run.

But I did.

I had sprinted towards the scene, rushing past all the pedestrians who were letting their morbid curiosity get the better of them and making it all the way to where the police tape was strung up before being stopped.

'You can't go through there,' a chubby, middle-aged policeman had told me, but that had barely slowed me down.

'Who is it?' I had demanded to know. 'Who has died?'

My question had been a dramatic one, and it had certainly taken the officer by surprise, but I had kept asking it until I got some semblance of an answer.

'A male in his thirties,' had been the eventual response, and that was when I knew for sure that it was my Paul in that bag.

It had to be. He was missing, and he never went missing. He would always come home to me. But now he hadn't, and here was a body bag lying right outside the place that he had been going to. It just had to be him. And that was why I had cried his name several times, not that he could hear me anymore but just because I wanted everybody standing around at the scene to know that I deserved to be allowed to get a little closer.

It had been my use of Paul's name that had got the attention of another officer at the scene, and she had rushed over to where I was still trying to get under the tape and asked me who I was.

'I'm Paul's girlfriend,' I had cried with tears in my eyes. 'Tell me that isn't him in there.'

I had pointed at the body bag then, aware how selfish my demand was because if it wasn't my loved one in there then it was somebody else's. But the policewoman had not been able to do what I wanted her to do. She hadn't made me feel a little better by telling me that I was mistaken and that the victim's name was not Paul. She had just looked incredibly sad before telling me that the I.D. in the victim's wallet had belonged to a Paul Barber.

My Paul Barber.

I don't remember too much about the next few minutes after that other than the policewoman telling me that an officer would have visited me, but they hadn't been able to find Paul's emergency contact in his phone or wallet. But that had hardly been a reassuring thing to hear and wouldn't have made the news any easier to take if it had come in the form of a polite knock on my front door.

Paul was dead.

His life was over.

And it felt like mine was too.

I don't know how long it has been since I watched the body bag get lifted off the concrete and taken away in an ambulance, nor do I know how long it has been since this policewoman has been talking to me at the station. All I know is that at some point, she is going to stop talking to me, and then all I will have left to do is go home to my empty house and be surrounded by Paul's belongings.

His clothes. His shoes. His stupid car magazines in the bathroom.

All of the things just stuck in the last place he left them, never to be touched by his hands again. Not only that, but there would be so many things that should have happened in that house that won't be happening anymore. He won't be lying in the bed with me. He won't be watching the television with me. And he won't be bringing me back any more snacks from the corner shop.

He lost his life on his way to get a couple of bags of crisps from a damn shop. How silly and pointless is that? I haven't processed much that the policewoman has said to me, but I did register the parts she told me about the man who hit my partner. Apparently, his name is Elliot, and he took his eyes off the road for one second before he hit Paul. I was told that Elliot is very shocked by what happened and deeply remorseful, but I'm not sure what I was supposed to do with that information. Can Elliot's shock and remorse bring Paul back? No, they can't, so, to be honest, I don't give a single damn about how Elliot is feeling now. He has taken another person's life, and even though it was an accident, he has still done it. A man is no longer breathing because of him. A man is no longer enjoying the gift of being in this world.

A man is no longer by my side.

The policewoman has told me that Elliot is in custody for causing death by dangerous driving and that the fact he has already admitted looking away from the road in front of him before hitting Paul means it's likely he will get sentenced in the end and serve time. But that didn't make me feel better either because locking up Elliot won't get me any closer to having Paul with me for the rest of my days. I don't care if he was doing seventy in a thirty zone, playing with his radio or drinking a four-pack of lager as he drove around town; the details don't matter.

I just want Paul back.

I've said just as much to the policewoman several times since I have been in this room at the station, as if my request is one she will somehow be able to help me with. But, of course, she cannot give me my boyfriend back because he is lying on a table somewhere being examined by people with fancy degrees in the human body. I am told that I will get to see Paul at some point but not just yet. For now, I am stuck here with this woman who is looking at me like she cannot even begin to imagine what I am going through.

She can't. Nobody can. I'm in a world of pain, and I don't think it will ever end now. How can it? What do I have to look forward to? Meeting somebody else? Falling in love again? No, I can't do that. Paul was the one for me, and we were madly in love with each other before he went. I can't just move on easily; it's not as simple as that. It's not as if he dumped me or had an affair or even just started to get on my nerves enough for me to leave him. We are separated forever now but not through choice. It's through sheer bad luck and some driver's split-second mistake.

Paul crossed a street. He expected to make it to the other side. But he didn't.

Now I'm expected to make it through the next few days with this pain in my body?

Just like my dear, deceased partner crossing that damn street to the corner shop, I don't think I'm going to be able to make it.

5

I'm dreading what is waiting for me on the other side of my front door when I open it and walk in over these next few seconds. It's something that is going to be a part of my home for a long time now. It's something that once might have seemed quite nice but now is going to haunt me with its relentlessness. It's something that will torture me all day and keep me awake all night.

It's silence.

The silence of living alone. The silence of nobody in the bed beside me.

The silence that reminds me that Paul is gone forever.

I'm dreading it so much that I can't even bring myself to put the key in the lock, so I leave that job to my sister, Ellen, who has accompanied me back home after spending the last several hours going through hell with me. I've been speaking to police officers and counsellors, all of whom have been offering me support and assuring me that I just need to "go home and rest" and "take it one day at a time." But not a single one of their words was of any consolation to me, and that was why I got them to call my sibling for support instead. Ellen is two years younger than me, but she has always been the more grown-up one out of the two of us. She got married in her early twenties, back when I was still sailing the seas of single life, and she is now the proud mother of two daughters, aged eight and six, and who are an absolute credit to her. She has the perfect family, and she has always been the perfect sister, which is why I needed her by my side today. Ellen is the only one who can help me get through this because she knows what I need and when I need it. Paul used to know those things too, but now I've lost him, I'm going to be leaning on my sister for support more than ever.

'Here we go,' Ellen says as she opens my front door and walks in ahead of me, flicking the switch on the wall in the hallway to give us some light so that we can see where we are going as we head inside.

Besides being dark, the house is cold, a result of nobody being home all day to turn the heating on. That means it's even more uninviting than it would normally be, and I feel as if my feet are made of lead as I step into my property and force myself to keep going.

'How about a cup of tea?' Ellen asks me as she closes the front door and turns the lock, a sign that she won't be leaving me alone this evening and has presumably already told her partner, Alex, that she won't be back tonight.

I just shrug at her suggestion as I stand uselessly by the staircase, and Ellen takes that as a 'yes' before she tells me to take a seat on the sofa in the living room while she puts the kettle on.

My sister moves a lot quicker than I do as she heads for the kitchen while I go into the living room, the one with the two sofas, although Paul and I really only ever sat on one, which was the one by the window where we would snuggle up and watch TV every night after work. But I can't bring myself to sit on that sofa now, so

I sit on the other one, the one that isn't quite as comfortable because my body isn't as familiar with it.

I hear the sound of cupboards and drawers being opened in the kitchen as Ellen gets to work on making us a drink while my vision drifts over to the bookcase to the left of the TV where several of Paul's books are on display. He wasn't a big reader, but he accumulated enough paperbacks over time to fill up a couple of shelves on this bookcase, and it's those books that my eyes are scanning over now. If he did read then he liked to read military fiction, the kind of stories where a weary ex-army veteran goes on some secretive mission to some foreign land and gets involved in all sorts of gunfights with dangerous villains. Sometimes, Paul would tell me what was happening in his books as he was sitting beside me in bed reading, and I would pretend to be interested in his macho fiction while reading my own book, which was usually an autobiography of some female celebrity that I found inspiring, but Paul found unbearable. We definitely had different tastes when it came to reading, and that's why this bookcase in front of me has such an eclectic mix of paperbacks on it. But it's not my books I'm looking at right now, it's his.

His books that will never be read again by their owner.

I was wrong about the thing I worried about before re-entering my home after Paul's death tonight. The silence isn't the worst part. The worst part is seeing my partner's possessions scattered around and knowing that he will never be back here to get any more use out of them. There's lots of things of his just in this room alone, besides the books on the shelves, and I'm starting to notice more and more of them as I look around. But I know that this is nothing compared to the number of things of his that are waiting for me upstairs. There are wardrobes and drawers full of his clothes in the bedroom, while one side of the sink in the bathroom is home to all his toiletries, like his toothbrush, his razor and his aftershave. Compared to seeing all of that, these books are relatively painless, and maybe that's because I know Paul hasn't touched any of these paperbacks in weeks. But he will have touched his toothbrush today when he brushed his teeth this morning, and it's mad how such a simple act has ended up being so significant.

The last time he ever brushed his teeth.

He wouldn't have known it at the time, and it would have just felt exactly the same as all the thousands of instances he would have done it before in his life, except it turned out to be the final time he would do it. Now that toothbrush is up there sitting in the cup, maybe even still wet from when Paul ran it under the tap before putting it back down and leaving the bathroom to start another day.

A day he would never get to finish.

'One cup of tea with two sugars. Get this inside you,' Ellen says as she enters the room carrying two cups, one of which she hands to me before taking a seat on the sofa beside me.

'Thanks,' I mutter, receiving the hot mug and feeling surprisingly reassured by the heat that is emanating from within it.

We sit in silence as we each take a sip of our drinks, but it's not a silence that needs to be filled quickly because I'm with my sister, not some stranger who might make me feel awkward. Ellen and I have grown up together, and we are as comfortable around each other as any other two human beings could be. But neither of us are perfect, and we are capable of making mistakes, and my sister has unfortunately just made a pretty big one right now. She could have given me any other cup in the cupboard to make me this tea, but she has inadvertently given me the one that has 'Best Boyfriend' emblazoned across the side of it. This was a gift from me to Paul one Christmas when I needed something cheap and simple to round out his gifts for that year, and I opted for this cheesy cup that I knew would make him smile. But it's not making me smile right now. It's just making me stare at it.

'Oh God, I'm so sorry!' Ellen cries when she realises her mistake. 'I wasn't looking at what I was doing! I'll get you another cup!'

She sits forward to try and take the cup from me, obviously mortified at what she has just done. But I shake my head and tell her that it's fine because while it was a shock, I don't want to hand this cup over and exchange it for another one. It's warm, and the tea inside it tastes good, but more than that, this cup has had Paul's hands wrapped around it countless times over the years. Somehow, holding on to it makes me feel a little closer to him, and I can almost trick my brain into imagining that the heat from within the mug is the warmth of his touch and not just the hot liquid inside.

'Why am I so stupid?' Ellen says, cursing her carelessness when it came to selecting me a cup just now, but that only makes me smile.

'You're not stupid. You just have no common sense.'

My sibling seems a little surprised by my ability to tease her in my tormented state, but I need a little slice of normality if I'm to stop myself going crazy, and there is nothing as normal to me as teasing my little sis.

'True,' she tells me with a self-deprecating nod, and I wait for her to come back with a tease of her own or just make some other kind of light-hearted comment that would tell me that things are normal and everything is going to be okay. But she doesn't do that, and I can hardly blame her because things aren't quite normal. The awkwardness that has never existed between us before has just emerged, and it's obviously because of what has gone on today. Ellen isn't being quiet because she is comfortable around me or because she is being respectful to me in my delicate state. She's being quiet because she doesn't know what to say to make things better. I guess I should let her know that there's no point even worrying about it because there's nothing that she can say to make things better right now.

I feel a wave of emotion coming over me and put my cup down quickly on the coffee table before I end up spilling it all over the sofa. Ellen is on hand to see how much I need her now, and she puts her cup down too before opening up her arms and accepting me into a tight hug.

Sobbing into her shoulder, I let my emotions pour out, and this is the first time I have properly wept since I saw that body bag lying in the road and realised that it was Paul inside it. I've spent most of the time since then stuck somewhere between shock and sad resignation, but now the tears are back, and it actually feels good to get them out. Ellen does her job as the supportive sister by holding me and giving me as long as I need to pull myself back together again, and by the time I do, the tea in our cups has gone cold. But neither of us care about that. We both just want this day to be over, and with the time approaching midnight, I guess it almost is.

'How about you try and have a lie down?' Ellen suggests when my sobs have tapered off into sniffles. 'I'll sleep in the spare bedroom, but just give me a shout if you need anything, okay?'

I nod my head before wiping my eyes and nose and forcing myself off the sofa where I have to make the short but difficult walk through my home, up the stairs and into the bedroom full of Paul's things. It's hard, and that's why I don't turn the light on in the bedroom when I get there, instead just flopping down onto the duvet and curling up in a ball, letting out some more tears and hoping that sleep will come for me quickly. But just before it does, I detect the scent of my late partner on his pillow next to my head, and it's as torturous a moment as any I have ever experienced in my life before.

Mercifully, I am asleep a few seconds later.

6

The advice of “take one day at a time” has been keeping me going throughout this first week of life without Paul by my side. I’ve been focused on following it so much that I’ve somehow been able to not only get through the ordeal of facing up to my partner’s death but also help organise his funeral. The sombre affair is taking place today, and it’s just one more thing to tick off a list that every grieving person has to go through.

But I suspect this will be the hardest thing to get through.

I spent a good half an hour staring at my reflection in the mirror this morning and looking at how my pale, white face contrasted with my deathly black clothing, and it was sobering to see how much of a toll the past seven days has taken on me. I looked drained of life, and I certainly felt it too. Now I’m making my way to the church where Paul is going to be laid to rest, passing by dozens of headstones that are dotted around in the graveyard to my left. Those people are buried and gone while I’m still here, but I feel as disconnected with life as they are now. I should be grateful to still be breathing and have the opportunity to look up at a cloudless sky and feel the warmth of the sun’s rays on my skin, but of course, I don’t. I feel as though I just want somebody to dig a hole for me in this graveyard too, so I can crawl into it and disappear down into the Earth, where I might finally find some peace. But I’m not the one going into the ground today, my boyfriend is, and I am here to say my final goodbye to him before his coffin is covered up forever.

Ellen is walking on my left-hand side, and her family are following behind us, as are my other relatives, which don't include my parents because they have passed away now. Several of my friends have also come here today to show their support, which is much appreciated, but we're outnumbered by how many people have come out from Paul's side here today to say their goodbyes. His family and friends are all making their way inside the church too, their heads bowed and their gaits slow and stiff, as if they are struggling to process how a man as full of life as Paul could be taken so early by such a silly thing as a driver who wasn't able to stop in time to avoid hitting a person crossing the street. The driver of that stupid car, Elliot, has been released on bail, but he's admitted to all the charges put to him, and it's thought that his sentencing will be a formality when his case eventually makes it before a judge. I will have to be present that day to see him given his fate, but it will be more for Paul than for me. I'd rather not see Elliot again, but I'll put myself through it to bring a little closure to the whole sorry episode. But today isn't about the man who took a life so needlessly. It's about the man who enhanced so many other people's lives.

Paul is going to be missed by a hell of a lot of people.

And right here is when those people get to prove it.

The following fifteen minutes are a blur of handshakes and condolences before I make it into my seat at the front of the church, staring solemnly at the box in front of me. I keep a tight grip on my sister's hand as the service begins, and the man standing in front of the mourners runs through the formalities, but all I am thinking about is how I am supposed to get up out of my seat and start speaking to the people here in a few moments' time. I felt it was important to put myself forward to say a few words today, considering that I was the person closest to Paul at the time of his death, but as the seconds tick by, I'm starting to think that I've bitten off more than I can chew. It's taking every ounce of my strength to not break down completely here, so I have no idea where I'm going to find the courage and composure to give a speech when I am eventually called to the front. I think my sister can sense this too because it doesn't take her long to lean in closer to me and whisper something in my ear.

'Do you want me to help with the speech?' she asks me, and I'm touched by her offer.

It takes me less than a second to give my response, and I nod my head eagerly, relieved that I won't have to try and get through it on my own.

By the time I get called to the front, I'm shaking a little, but Ellen is more than up to the task of supporting me, and it's actually her who begins the speech, so I have an extra few seconds to try and compose myself.

'I'm Sarah's sister, Ellen,' she begins, introducing herself for the benefit of some of Paul's friends here today who might not know who she is. 'My sister is going to say a few words shortly, but before she does, I just want to say what a pleasure it was to have a man like Paul in my family's life. He was a gentleman with a wicked sense of humour, and there is no doubt that my sister did well when it came to having him as a boyfriend.'

I take a deep breath and look up at the faces of the people staring in our direction, and I see several of them smiling at the kind words Ellen has just offered, as well as several people dabbing at their bleary eyes with tissues and looking as bad as I feel. I try to focus on the smiles and not the sobs as Ellen goes on, and the more that I do, the more I find myself building up the courage to offer my own sentiments when my sister eventually stops speaking.

The silence that descends on the church a few minutes' later lets me know that Ellen has finished, and I turn to look at her before I begin, needing one final boost of confidence from my sibling before I proceed. I get it in the form of a warm smile from her kind face, and now I am ready to get this over with.

'I never imagined I would ever have to stand here and do something like this,' I begin, swallowing hard as I finish speaking as a way to try and ease my dry throat because there isn't any water to hand. 'But then again, I never imagined meeting somebody like Paul either.'

I see more friendly faces giving me encouragement to keep going, so I do.

'He was a wonderful partner. He was my best friend. And he was the person I wanted to spend the rest of my life with. And now he is gone and all because he went to the shop on a Sunday morning to get me a packet of crisps.'

I say the last part in a light-hearted way as if it's some kind of silly joke that will make everybody laugh and ease some of the tension in the room. But it doesn't exactly come out like that, and it only ends up serving to remind both me and the rest of the mourners here of how frighteningly unpredictable life can be.

'I wish he had stayed in bed with me that morning,' I go on, wiping a tear from my eye. 'I wish I'd told him that I didn't need anything from the shop and that I already had everything I needed right there in bed with me because I did. Paul was everything to me, and I just hope that he knew that.'

I see several people nod their heads as if they are letting me know that Paul did know how much I cared about him, and they include Paul's parents, who are sitting on the front row and who look as if they have aged twenty years since the last time I visited their house with their son by my side. But the fact they are nodding at what I have just said tells me that they know I made their son happy while he was alive and that I'm not at all to blame for what ended up happening to him.

I wrap up my speech by telling Paul's spirit that I will always love him and cherish the time we had together before reaching out and touching the side of the coffin as if it is my way of being close to him one final time before he is carried away and put in the ground.

Then Ellen helps me back to my seat, and I'm able to stay strong enough to make it through the rest of the service before the pallbearers get out of their seats and begin their slow, long march to take my boyfriend away forever.

Then I can't do it anymore.

Then I finally break down, and this time, the tears feel as though they will never stop flowing.

7

It's been two days since I said goodbye to Paul amongst the rows of gravestones at that church where Ellen spoke so eloquently while I just fumbled my way through my own speech. I've spent those two days sitting in my house and trying to bring myself to start going through Paul's things, so I can get this place more organised for the future, but I've not got very far. I've spent time looking at some of my boyfriend's belongings, but I haven't thrown a single thing away, and I'm not sure I will ever be able to. I get what the counsellor is telling me about how it will help me move on going forward if I stop surrounding myself with memories of what I have lost, but it's still far too soon for anything like that. Right now, I just want to wallow in my grief, and that means keeping everything that Paul owned close to me, so I feel as though he is still somehow close to me too.

Ellen has visited to make me the cups of tea that are quickly becoming the only highlight of my existence, but I am currently alone, lying on my bed and looking at old photos on my phone. They are mostly pictures that I took during my time with Paul, and there are plenty of images that are making me smile right now, like the one of us on holiday in Portugal last year. We looked so tanned, happy and in love, and I'd give anything to go back to that time in the Algarve now. But it's not just holiday photos that are documented here. There are plenty of pictures taken much closer to home, like the picnic in the park we had a couple of summers ago or the time we took a day trip to Bath and had great fun in the picturesque city.

I've lost track of time going through all of these, and I could probably spend the rest of the evening doing so if it wasn't for the email notification that I suddenly receive that has me opening up my inbox to check it out.

As I go in search of the new message, I am assuming it will either be spam or an email from one of the many retail stores I subscribe to, offering me huge discounts on their summer sale. Those kinds of emails tend to make up around 90% of the messages that go into my inbox on a daily basis. But to my surprise, the new email is not spam or sales related. Instead, it's telling me that my email from the future has arrived.

My stomach lurches when I see the title of the email because I know exactly what this is and why I have just received it. Six months ago, I went onto a website in which users can write themselves a message and then pick a date on which they will receive that message in the future. The idea behind it is that you write down exactly what you want to be happening in your life by that future date and then instruct the website to send you that message at some point ahead of time. I chose six months, and I guess the six months has just elapsed.

It seemed like a silly thing to do at the time, but I had heard about it from a woman at work who had done something similar, and she had recommended it. Her mother had been going through a battle with cancer, so she had gone onto this website and written down that in six months' time, her mother's cancer would be in remission, and everything would be well again in the family. The woman had gone on to completely forget about what she had done, but then the email popped up in her inbox one day, and when she read it, it had reduced her to tears because everything she had wished for within it had come true. Her mother was in remission, and things were looking brighter for the family's future. Obviously, that was more down to the hard work of the medical staff at the hospital that had been treating her mother rather than the magic of an email from the past, but my colleague still believed that there was something in asking the universe for something and putting it out into the future. I thought it sounded fun, if a little quirky, so I had gone home that night and had a go at it myself. I had written myself a message of what I wanted to be happening in my life in six months' time. And then I had pressed send.

That message is now staring back at me from my phone screen, and my eyes scan over it as I read its contents.

On this day in six months, I will be engaged to Paul Barber, and we will be planning our wedding. I can't wait!

I feel as if somebody has punched me in the stomach as I read the words, not because they are a surprise to me but because I know that unlike my colleague and her sick mother, my vision for the future has not come true. There will be no engagement or wedding with Paul now, and this will be just one of the many dreams I have had in my life that has failed to materialise in the real world.

I had forgotten that I'd sent this message to myself half a year ago, but now that it's here, I do remember writing it. I was sitting on my bed in this exact position at the time, and I had done it while Paul was in the bathroom so that he wouldn't know what I was writing. It would have been very awkward for me if he had seen this because it would have put him on the spot when it came to popping the question or not, and I didn't want that. But the fact that I wrote this when I could have written anything else in the world lets me know now just how important it was to me that I one day became the new Mrs Barber.

I wipe a tear from my eye as I re-read the message, but then a thought occurs to me, and it's one that changes my mood from a downbeat one to one filled with a little hope. I know that Paul is gone now, and he is never coming back, but I also know that I told him about this 'write your future' website at the time, and he said he was going to do a message of his own. Now that I think of it, I remember him taking out his own laptop and sitting beside me on the bed while he typed out his own message for six months' time, and although he didn't show me what he had written because it was a secret, he definitely pressed send on it. That means if I have got this message today in my inbox then he would have got one in his inbox as well.

It isn't going to bring my partner back, but suddenly, the thought that I could learn what he was hoping to have happening in his life half a year later when he wrote that message is enough to give me a feeling of excitement that I haven't had at all since he died. What if I could read what Paul had written? What if I knew what his hopes and dreams were too? Maybe it would be a source of comfort for me in this difficult time. I'm willing to try anything to make myself feel better now and get myself through another lonely night, and that's why I get up off the bed and go in search of Paul's laptop, determined to find it, log on and see what my beloved boyfriend wished for his future.

It takes me a while to locate his laptop in the house, but I eventually find it on a chair under the table in the dining room, and when I do, I open up the screen and press the power button. The laptop goes through its process of loading up, and as it does, my mind is racing with thoughts of all of the things that Paul might have written in his email to himself.

Did he mention me? Did he mention marriage? Was he really happy with the life he had made for himself, or did he want more?

I can't wait to find out, and it feels as if this is a way for me to have some new communication with him from beyond the grave. But then I see the icon pop up in the centre of the screen that tells me to enter the password to log on.

And that's when I realise that I have no idea what it is.

8

There's a reason why passwords exist. They're supposed to prevent unauthorised persons from accessing information that doesn't belong to them. That is the same reason why I now cannot log onto Paul's laptop to check his emails and see what he sent to himself six months ago. It's because that information doesn't belong to me, so I don't have the necessary credentials to see it.

But that doesn't mean I'm not trying.

So far, I have tried seventeen different passwords that I have guessed may have been used by my late partner, but none of them have worked, and worse, I have no idea if I have even been close. The screen I am working on doesn't tell me if I was 'hot' or 'cold' with my attempts. It simply says **'Incorrect password'** and leaves it up to me to decide if I want to have another go again.

I could give up, and I perhaps should, but trying to get onto Paul's laptop is at least providing me with a temporary distraction from all the pain and suffering I was going through while I was lying on the bed upstairs looking at our old photos. I needed something else to occupy my mind, however trivial, and this task right here has provided me with that. I might never be able to get into his emails and see what he wrote in the past, but at least I'll pass some time until tiredness overwhelms me again and mercifully allows me to sleep for a few precious hours before I wake up and get reminded of the mess my life is in.

Having another go, I enter a variation on one of the passwords I have already tried, which is Paul's favourite football team, followed by some numbers that have some relevance to him, but that doesn't work either. When I first sat down here and attempted to 'crack the code,' part of me would have felt a little disappointed if his password had turned out to be related to sport rather than to do with me, but now I don't care. I won't be offended by the fact that he used something other than my name, birthday or date we met to keep his laptop secure, all I want is to be able to access it. But I continue to have no luck, and the longer I go on, the more I realise how futile this is. I'm never going to be able to guess Paul's password. Even if I can land on the right subject, there is still no way I can know what numbers and symbols he might have used alongside it. The way passwords work these days, computer users are encouraged to press the most random sequence of keys before their security is set, so I've not got much chance of breaking this. In the end, the knock on my front door is a relief because it stops me from wasting any more time going down a dead-end path.

It's nine o'clock at night, and I don't usually receive visitors at my house at this time, but I have a feeling about who it might be on the other side of my door. My assumption is right when I open it and see Ellen standing on my doorstep with a smile on her face and another box of tea bags under her arm.

'Hey, I thought you might be running low, so I brought these around,' she tells me as she flashes me the teabags before stepping inside without waiting for an invitation because that's just what sisters do when they visit each other.

'I'm only running low because you keep coming here and making me so many cups of tea,' I say as I close the front door, and Ellen laughs as she takes off her coat, clearly here for more of a visit than just to drop off some supplies.

'You know, you don't have to make up an excuse if you want to come around and check that I'm okay,' I tell her as I lead her into the kitchen, determined to be the one to put the kettle on this time. 'You can just visit without teabags.'

'I'm not making up an excuse,' Ellen tries, but she knows I'm not buying it, and she gives me a wink as she takes a seat at my kitchen counter and allows me to make her a drink for the first time in a while.

I expect she is taking the sight of me catering to her as a promising sign that I am slowly recovering from what I have been through, but it's just pouring hot water from a kettle into a cup and adding a dash of milk. I can still do a simple task like that with a broken heart, although only just.

'So, how's it going?' Ellen asks me after I have given her a drink and taken a seat beside her.

'Crap, but slightly less crap than it was yesterday,' I say, being as honest as I can.

'I'm proud of you for being so strong, sis.'

'I'm not being strong, I'm just surviving.'

'I know. But whatever you have to do to get through this, I am proud of you for doing it.'

I smile weakly at my sibling before taking a sip of my tea, and despite the fact that I was able to make it, I haven't done a very good job. It's not great, and Ellen's facial expression says it when she takes a sip of her own a few seconds later.

'I think I'll make the next cup,' she tells me, and I can't help but laugh, which is an act that feels incredibly unusual to me at that moment, as well as makes me worry that I'm betraying Paul by finding it in myself to do such a thing at a time like this. But I know he wouldn't care about that. He would want me to be happy, not wallowing in misery, and I know Ellen just wants the same thing for me too.

'I've been trying to get onto Paul's laptop,' I say as I push my cup of weak tea away and run my hand over my tired face.

'What are you doing that for?'

'I don't know. I just thought there might be some things on there that will cheer me up.'

I can see by my sister's facial expression that she isn't convinced.

'I'm not sure that's a good idea. Aren't you just tormenting yourself?'

'No, I'm not.'

'Didn't the counsellor say it would be better to not go through his things because it makes you dwell on the pain instead of looking to the future?'

'The counsellor said a lot of things, but at the end of the day, I'm the one going through this, not her.'

'I know, but she's just trying to help.'

'I get it, but everyone is trying to help me, and I'm not sure everybody knows what is really best for me. All I know is that going through Paul's things is making me feel better right now, and that's enough to get me through to tomorrow.'

Ellen seems to accept that answer, even if she still isn't sure about what I'm doing.

'So, what did you find on his laptop?'

'Nothing. I can't log on to it.'

'You two didn't share passwords?'

'Nope.'

'Oh, that's a bummer.'

Ellen takes another sip from her cup but then quickly remembers that she had stopped drinking from it because of how bad it tastes, and I laugh at her mistake as she screws up her face.

'Do you and Alex tell each other your passwords?' I ask her about her husband, wondering if that is actually a normal thing for couples to do.

'Yeah, although it took a bit of convincing to get him to want to do it.'

'I never even thought to try and find out Paul's passwords when he was alive. I guess I trusted him.'

'Oh, don't get me wrong. I trust Alex too. It's just that it's still nice to know that I could go snooping if I wanted to, and he can do the same thing. Not that we ever do.'

I nod my head and wish I had done the same thing with Paul now because I'd be able to access his laptop instead of being frustrated by the incorrect password message every ten seconds.

'What is it you're looking for on there anyway?' Ellen asks me.

'Nothing, it's silly,' I say, feeling a little embarrassed about the whole 'write your future' thing, but I have a feeling she isn't going to let me leave it there.

'I've come here tonight, and you've made me a rubbish cup of tea. The least you can do is tell me what you're looking for on the laptop.'

I laugh again and see that Ellen is pleased with that reaction because she is mainly here to get me back to being the woman I used to be before I was struck by tragedy. Then I decide that I might as well tell her because it's pretty harmless.

'Six months ago, Paul and I went on this website where you write a message about how you want your life to be in six months, and then they send you the same message by email when the time has passed. I was hoping to get into his emails and see what he wrote to himself.'

'What did you write to yourself?'

I pause before answering because I feel like thinking about it will put me at risk of tears again, and I haven't cried for at least an hour now, but I have to tell her.

'I said that I wanted to be engaged to Paul and to be planning our wedding.'

Ellen stares at me as she processes my response, and I can see that she has no idea what to say to that. Obviously, it's not a great thing to hear that your sister dreamt of being engaged to her boyfriend in six months and instead, she has just watched that boyfriend be buried in a grave.

‘I told you it was silly,’ I say, batting the air with one of my hands to let her know to ignore it and move on. But she doesn’t, and this time, it looks like she is the one who is about to cry.

‘Oh, sis, I’m so sorry,’ she says, and she opens up her arms for me to come to her and have a hug.

‘It’s fine,’ I lie as I go into her arms, but the tears are stinging at my eyes again, and now we are both crying.

‘This isn’t fair. You and Paul were made for each other,’ Ellen says as we keep hugging, and I have to agree with her. But what can I do? In the end, I just say nothing.

By the time we break off from the hug, we’re both sporting bloodshot eyes and sniffling like silly little children, which is quite the look for a pair of women in their thirties. But I feel better for letting out a little more of my pain, and I think Ellen does too.

‘I don’t think you should try and get on Paul’s laptop,’ she tells me after drying her eyes and wiping her nose. ‘Even if you can get on his emails, it’ll be too painful to see what he wrote about the future.’

As much as I don’t want to admit it, I know my sister is right, and I nod my head to let her know that I will take her advice. Then I tell her that I’m tired and could do with a lie down, so she gathers up her things and heads for the front door, making me promise that I will call her if I need anything as she goes. I tell her that I will before wishing her goodnight and going around the downstairs rooms to turn off the lights before bed. But as I turn off the dining room light, I see the glow from the open laptop screen on the table where the password bar is still showing and inviting me to have another go at beating it.

But I'm not going to try and do that.

I'm going to save myself the pain.

I'm just going to go to bed and tick off another day since Paul left me.

9

The darkness in my bedroom is strangely comforting. I suppose not being able to see anything is helpful when there are so many things you don't want to see. If the light was on then I would surely still be looking at Paul's things, and that would be making me feel worse. But with the light off, the only thing I can see is a hint of pale moonlight peeking around the edges of the closed curtain, and that is soothing for me.

The only problem I have now is that I can't sleep.

I've been lying here for hours with my body curled up tightly on my side of the bed, almost afraid to stray onto the empty side because that would feel as if I am intruding on Paul's space and acknowledging the fact that he will never be here to fill it again. For some reason, I feel as if it is important that I keep within that invisible boundary line down the centre of the bed that all couples try and keep within when they are sharing a mattress, although in my case now, there is no reason why I can't spread out and take up some more room.

It's funny, but I used to love sleeping alone. I'd stretch out my legs diagonally, and many times I would wake up in a sleeping position that can only be described as 'The Starfish.' But all that changed when I got into a serious relationship because one of the first things to go when that happens is the novelty of having a bed to yourself. Suddenly, my space had been cut in half, and I had to contend with errant elbows and knees on the other side of the bed, never mind a little snoring every once in a while too. But that's a small price to pay to be able to end a day and start the next one beside the person you love.

I loved sharing a bed with Paul and not just because of naughty reasons. I loved it because I could lie on his chest and listen to his heartbeat. I loved it because I could feel his arm wrap around my waist, as I dozed on my side. And I loved it because no matter what had happened in the sixteen or so hours since we had last lied down together, things always felt better when we were side by side again and falling asleep.

Now it's just me on my own in the darkness, and I guess that is why sleep is hopelessly out of reach for me.

I could keep lying here and stubbornly keep my eyes closed, but I'm not sure how much good it will do, so I decide to kill a few more minutes of this long night by getting out of bed and creeping into the bathroom, although I'm not sure what I am creeping for. There's nobody else in the house but me, so I'm not in danger of waking anybody, but I guess it's just a habit I formed over ten years of trying not to wake my sleeping boyfriend.

Having relieved myself and washed my hands while managing not to glance down at Paul's toothbrush by the sink, I am almost back to my bed when I stupidly stub my toe on the edge of the wardrobe.

'Damn it!' I cry out, the frustration and pain rising out of me uncontrollably and leaving me hopping around the dark room on one leg like a drunk pirate.

My eyes are watering, and my teeth are gritted, but most of all, I'm just angry. Angry at the stupid wardrobe. Angry at my stupid, weak toe. And angry at the fact this is about as good as my night is going to get.

Falling onto the bed because I can't bear to put my injured foot down on the carpet, I reach over and turn on the bedside lamp and then lie there as my heart rate slowly comes back down and my eyes stop watering. My toe is still throbbing, and I expect it will be for quite some time, but everything else around my body is slowly going back to normal. But with the light on, I am now able to see everything again, and Paul's possessions stare back at me from their various locations around the room, almost taunting me with the memory of the life I used to have.

This is it, I decide as I force myself up off the bed and head over to the first thing I can see of Paul's, which happens to be a pair of jeans hanging over the back of a cabinet. *It's time to follow the advice of the counsellor and start clearing out some of my late boyfriend's things.*

I work surprisingly efficiently for a woman with a dodgy toe at half-three in the morning, and it doesn't take me long to have sorted Paul's errant items of clothing into a neat pile on the bed. Throwing them away or donating them to charity feels like far too big of a step to take at this time, but I can at least ensure they are out of sight, so I open the wardrobe that belonged to my boyfriend and put the clothes on the top shelf.

Out of sight, out of mind?

Yeah, right, but at least I'm trying now.

I go to close the wardrobe door but realise it's jamming now, and that's because a pair of Paul's jeans has slipped down and is currently blocking the door.

Bending over to pick the jeans up, my hands grip the smart denim material, and that's how I feel something lumpy in the back pocket.

I'm curious as to what it could be, so I reach into the pocket and take it out, and that's when I see that it is a brown leather wallet.

There wouldn't be anything particularly unusual about finding a wallet in a man's jeans, but this gets my attention because I know what wallet Paul used to use for everything, and it didn't look like this one. He used a black leather wallet with his initials on it because that was the one I gave him as a Christmas present two years ago. I have never seen this brown wallet before, and while it is presumably one of his old ones, I open it up to take a look inside and check.

Exploring the contents of the wallet, I find a couple of debit cards that are presumably linked to his bank accounts, although I would have thought he kept his cards in the wallet he used on a daily basis. I also find £70 in cash, which would suggest he has used this wallet recently because who would leave a decent amount of money somewhere it would never be spent? But other than the cards and cash, I can't see anything else, and I'm just about to close the wallet when a small slip of paper falls out of it.

Crouching down to pick it up off the carpet, I open the piece of paper up and see that there is a long line of letters and numbers handwritten across it. It seems like an inconsequential sequence and doesn't make any sense if it was to be read in a traditional manner, but then I realise what it does look like.

It looks like a password.

My mind instantly goes back to the laptop that is still sitting on the dining room table, the laptop that I wasted time trying to log into earlier. I wonder would I be able to access it if I was to try and input the letters and numbers on this piece of paper?

It has to be worth a try.

Going downstairs in my bare feet with the piece of paper in my hand, I reach the dining room and turn on the light before taking a seat in the chair in front of the laptop.

I'm just about to have a go at entering the password I have found when I remember what my sister told me after she called around earlier.

"I don't think you should try and get on Paul's laptop. Even if you can get on his emails, it'll be too painful to see what he wrote about the future."

Her words make me internally debate the decision as to whether or not I proceed from here, but I decide that I might as well try because the chances are this isn't the password anyway, and I won't be able to log in regardless.

Putting my fingers on the keyboard, I cross-reference the piece of paper as I enter the sequence written on it and then my finger hovers over the ENTER key when I am done.

I take a deep breath before pressing it, but when I do, I expect to see the same message I saw before.

'Incorrect Password.'
Only I don't.
It seems I have successfully logged in.

10

It's easy enough to navigate my way through the internal system on Paul's laptop because I've used enough computers in my time, and they're all pretty much the same to a layman like me. That's why it doesn't take me too long to find the icon that will open up my late boyfriend's emails. But I haven't clicked that icon yet, and the reason for that is the screensaver staring me right in the face.

It's a photo of Paul and I on a night out.

We look so young and fresh-faced, as well as a little drunk, and I know exactly when this picture was taken. It was in the winter of 2015, at my work's Christmas party. Employees had been allowed to invite their partners back in those days before budget cuts and other boring things ruined the fun for everybody, and it had been great to have Paul with me as I celebrated the end of another working year. We had danced and drunk lots with my colleagues, as well as wrapped tinsel around our heads and pulled a stupid face, which is exactly what this photo on Paul's laptop depicts now.

I stare at the screensaver for several long moments, studying every inch of it and feeling all of the happiness and drunken joy I felt in the moment it was taken. *If only we knew then what we know now.* Both of us look like we didn't have a care in the world, and that was exactly how it should be. Now the man with the tinsel around his head in the photo is gone forever, and the woman with the tinsel around her head doesn't feel like she'll ever get back to being that carefree person again.

Forcing myself to click the icon at the bottom of the screen that will open Paul's emails, I feel a little better once the screensaver is out of view. Now I am just looking at a long list of unread emails, and it's not quite as galling as the old photo. Scanning over the subject lines of the emails, I see that some of them are work-related ones that he must have forwarded from his company account to work on at home, while the rest are just mailing list newsletters that he has signed up to over the years. All of this is to be expected and also very sad because he obviously won't ever be opening any of these messages, never mind responding to them. But I'm not here to snoop around in another person's inbox too much, even if I was very closely connected to that person. I'm just here to see if I can find the message that he wrote to himself six months ago.

Clicking on the search bar in the top right-hand corner of the screen, I enter the name of the website that we both used to play the silly game of 'writing our future'. Then I hit ENTER and let the search engine do its thing, trawling through all of my boyfriend's emails to hopefully land on the only one I am looking for.

It doesn't take long for it to produce the result that I wanted, and I double-click the solitary unread message that now appears on my screen, opening it up for myself when really it was only ever supposed to be read by Paul.

The colourful banner across the header of the email is recognisable as the same one that was on the email I received, and I scroll down a little to get to the message.

I can tell immediately that it is a little longer than the message I wrote and seems to be broken up into parts, rather than just one concise sentence. I'm surprised by that because I hadn't realised Paul would have taken this so seriously and had so much to say. I thought he was just humouring me when he agreed to do it. But I guess he did have a few hopes and dreams of his own for the future, and now it's time to find out what they were.

Without further ado, I take a deep breath and begin reading.

On this day in six months, I will still be in a great relationship with Sarah, and we will be stronger than ever.

I beam at the first part of his message because it's clear from this that he loved me just as much as I loved him, and that's all I could ask for. Okay, so he didn't dream of being engaged in six months like I did in my message, but I can't complain about what he chose to write. It's so sweet and as soul-crushing as it is to know that he is now gone, I can take some solace in the fact that our relationship really was stronger than ever just before he passed.

Then I move onto the second part of his message.

On this day in six months, Chelsea will be top of the league and playing some amazing football.

I laugh out loud at Paul's silly wish because it is so him. I should have known he would put something about football in here. He was a big Chelsea fan and went to as many games as he could when I wasn't dragging him around a shopping centre on a Saturday afternoon instead, of course. I'm not quite sure where Chelsea are in the league right now because I don't exactly keep abreast of things like that, but however well they are doing, they have definitely lost a good fan in Paul.

Then I move onto the third part of his message.

On this day in six months, I will be feeling a lot better about my past.

I re-read that part four or five times to try and make some sense of it, but I have absolutely no idea what Paul could mean by that. Feeling better about his past? What past? I'm not aware of any troubles or traumas in his past, so I have no idea what he could be referring to here, but there was obviously something bothering him, and I wish I knew what it was.

Leaning back in my seat, I rack my brains for anything I can think of that might explain what this could mean, but I can't come up with anything. The only thing I can think of doing is asking his parents if they know what he could be talking about here. I wouldn't have to let on that I had accessed his emails and seen some silly message he had written to his future self to do that. I could just ask them if there was anything in the past that had been troubling their son, and I guess I'll have to because that's probably the only way I have a chance of finding out what this means.

I am puzzled by the past thing, but there is still one more sentence to read in Paul's message, so I lean forward again to be closer to the screen so that I can see it.

And then I read the words that will change everything forever.

On this day in six months, I will have ended things with Fiona.

Wait, what?

What does that mean?

Who the hell is Fiona?

11

It's now sunlight instead of moonlight that is seeping through the curtains of my home, and that tells me that I have been sat at this laptop for hours. But there is a good reason for that, and there's also a good reason why I'm not planning on going anywhere for a few more hours yet. I'm trying to find anything and everything I can on Paul's laptop that might give me some indication as to who Fiona was.

The sentence ***On this day in six months, I will have ended things with Fiona*** could mean anything, but the human brain has a nasty habit of automatically assuming the worst, and that is why I am now thinking that my beloved boyfriend might have been cheating on me. Ending things with another woman sure does give off the impression that there is some kind of a relationship to end. After all, you can't end something if nothing exists.

So is that the case? Was Paul having an affair with somebody called Fiona?

I don't know yet, but it's what I have to find out.

Maybe my sister was right. Maybe I shouldn't have tried accessing my boyfriend's personal things. But now that I have, there is no going back. I've opened Pandora's Box, and there is no closing it again until I have set my mind at ease. The only way I will do that is by finding out exactly what my partner meant when he said that he wanted to have ended things with somebody called Fiona.

The first thing I did after learning the name of the mystery woman was type it into the search bar on Paul's emails and press ENTER. I wanted to see if there had been any correspondence between my boyfriend and a woman going by this name, and I expected any results I got to shine some light on this confusing situation. But the search engine had other ideas, and it failed to return me a single result for 'Fiona', which either meant that she had never emailed my partner before, or he had just deleted it after reading.

With the emails not helping me anymore, I ventured into other parts of the laptop, searching through files and folders for anything with the name 'Fiona' in it. But while I do know my way around a computer, I'm by no means an I.T. geek, so perhaps there were faster ways of searching than the ones I was able to come up with. It has taken me a long time to search through the hard drive on this laptop to find anything of interest, and as of yet, I haven't got anything. Not a single mention of the name Fiona anywhere on this device.

I rub my bleary eyes and think about getting up to make a coffee, but that would mean leaving my workstation, and I'm far too engaged on my task to do that. Instead, I go onto the internet and make my way to a search engine that never fails to provide answers.

It's time to use my trusty old friend called Google.

I know that I obviously can't just type in 'Fiona' here and expect to find anything worthwhile to my search, but that doesn't mean that I can't use this handy bit of technology to assist me in accessing the deepest recesses of my late boyfriend's laptop. Typing into the search bar beneath the colourful and very familiar logo, I ask this search engine to tell me how to find out a person's contact details if they are stored on a laptop that is the same make and model as the one I am sitting in front of right now.

Google does its job, thousands of times in fact, but I only need telling once, so I click the first result on the page and then see my screen fill with a short checklist of what a person is to do if they are trying to accomplish what I am trying to do.

Committing the first few steps in the checklist to my memory, I leave the webpage and return to the desktop screen on the laptop before searching for the name of the application that stores contacts on this device. I find it easily enough and then use the rest of the checklist to make sure I know what to do once it has opened up.

Now I am looking at the place where Paul could have kept the contact details of anybody he wanted to, and while there is no guarantee that Fiona will be in here, I might as well have a look.

I type her name into the toolbar, feeling extremely nervous as I do because I'm not sure what I really want to achieve with this. Do I want her contact details to pop up in a few seconds' time or not? If they do, then it will only confirm that my boyfriend was friendly with somebody called Fiona, and that will add more mystery and intrigue to what he could have meant in his message. But if I don't find anything, then I'll be no closer to knowing the truth, although it might make it less likely that he was having an affair if he didn't have a contact by that name.

In the end, I just put myself out of my misery and press ENTER.

And then I find myself staring at Fiona's phone number.

My eyes are blinking almost as quickly as the cursor on the laptop screen as I stare at the line of digits in front of me. So Paul did know somebody called Fiona. Is this the Fiona he referenced in his ominous message to himself six months ago? It could very well be, and I guess there is only one way to find out.

I need to call the number.

But I'm not moving a muscle. I'm not reaching for my phone or preparing to speak to this mystery person. Instead, I'm just staying perfectly still and trying not to think the worst. It's easy enough to do that now because I don't know too much yet. All I know is that Paul was *maybe* having an affair. Maybe is a comforting word because it allows for the possibility that a better outcome can be achieved. Maybe is a much better word than *definitely* because that word doesn't leave any room for doubt, and right now, doubt is my best friend. If I am doubting this then it still means that there is a chance of Paul being the perfect man I thought he was. As long as I can doubt then I can cling on to my happy past with him. But if I pick up the phone, speak to Fiona and find out she was the other woman in my man's life then everything I thought I knew is gone for good.

All the 'I love you's' that Paul whispered to me before we fell asleep each night.

All the assurances that he would never leave me, no matter what might happen in the future.

And all the occasional innocent daydreams of us one day perhaps getting married, having a family and growing old together.

All gone. *If* I make this phone call and ask Fiona how she knew my late boyfriend.

I get up out of my seat and walk away from the phone number on the laptop screen, but I'm not going in search of my mobile. I'm going into the kitchen to make myself that coffee that I've been putting off for too long. I need a hit of caffeine, and I need it before I can plan my next move because no good plan was ever made with a weary mind after a sleepless night. I need a legal drug to pick me up, and then I need to figure out what I will do next. But as I wait for the kettle to boil, I already feel like I know who I need to speak to, and it isn't Fiona, at least not yet anyway.

It's Ellen.

My sister will know what to do in this situation because she always knows what to do. I tease her about her lack of common sense, but she is always on the ball when it comes to more serious things, and I'm not sure there are many more serious things than potential infidelity in a loving relationship. I could ask her for her opinion on this, getting her to read Paul's message and see if she jumps to the same troubling conclusion that I first jumped to. Perhaps she will read it differently and come up with a perfectly reasonable explanation for what it could mean. It's possible because she won't be as emotionally invested in it as I am. I'm far too close to this thing to be objective. I'm grieving. I'm confused. And I'm jealous because Fiona might be a love rival of mine. That means I am hardly the best person to be coming to rational conclusions.

I'll have my coffee, and then I will go and see my sister. It's Sunday, so she'll be home. Then I will tell her everything that I have found.

Then I will see what she thinks I should do next.

12

I ring the doorbell on my sister's front door, confident that it is now late enough in the morning to not risk waking up my two nieces inside. I'm not quite sure what time they get out of bed these days because it seems to be as variable as the wind, at least according to their mother anyway, but it's gone nine o'clock, so they must be up. Sure enough, they are because I see two small, smiling faces staring back at me when the door opens and as sleepy, stressed and sorrowful as I am, it can't fail to bring a small smile to my own face.

'Hi, Auntie Sarah!' cries Molly, the eight-year-old.

'Auntie Sarah, yay!' cries Bethany, the six-year-old.

'Hi girls, how are you?' I reply as I step into the house, and they both give me a hug, their little arms wrapping around my waist and legs and making me feel very loved.

It's a different kind of love to the one I felt with Paul, but it's no less powerful and magical, and despite what I have lost recently, I know I am still incredibly lucky to have a family like this.

'Auntie Sarah! Will you come and look at the painting I have done?' Molly asks me, pulling my left hand in the direction of the kitchen.

'Auntie Sarah! Will you come and play upstairs with me?' Bethany asks, pulling my right hand in the direction of the staircase.

I'm going to be split in two by this pair of eager youngsters if I'm not careful, so I tell them that I will do what they want me to later, but first I need to speak to their mummy.

'She's in the garden,' Molly tells me.

'What's she doing out there?' I ask as I go through the hallway in the direction of the back door, but before I can get there, I see my brother-in-law rushing down the stairs looking very harassed.

'I told you not to answer the door until I got there!' he calls down to his daughters as he fastens up the button on his jeans, and I presume he was in the bathroom having a peaceful moment before the doorbell rang and his daughters went wild.

'Hey, Alex,' I say as he sees me standing in the hallway below him. 'How's it going?'

'Oh, hey, Sarah! Good. How are you?'

His movements suddenly become very stiff and awkward, almost as if he doesn't know what to do with himself now that he knows I am here, and I expect it is to do with the fact that he doesn't really feel comfortable being around a woman who has just lost her partner. He was very quiet at the funeral, mainly keeping to one side and playing with the girls, while Ellen stayed with me and helped me through the day. I guess that was what he needed to do as a father, but I expect he was also glad to be out of the way too because then it meant that he didn't have to engage in too many awkward conversations with me, much like the one we are about to have right now.

'I'm okay, thanks,' I reply, lying but not wanting to be too downbeat in front of my nieces. 'How are things with you?'

'Yeah, good,' he says before catching himself and changing his mind. 'Well, not good with everything's that's happened lately. You know what I mean. I'm okay. We're okay. Erm…'

I smile at Alex because he is obviously trying his best, but he's better at being a dad than he is at making small talk with his grieving sister-in-law, so I tell him that I need to speak to his wife in the garden, and he takes the hint and takes over looking after the girls.

'Let me know when you're ready to play!' Bethany calls after me as I walk away, and I tell her that I will, before stepping out of the back door and spotting my sister down at the bottom of the garden.

'What are you up to, sis?' I say as I approach Ellen, and she jumps a little, seemingly startled at my sudden appearance.

'Sarah! I didn't know you were here!' she replies, and she walks up the lawn towards me, not answering my question, probably because she wasn't doing anything. I know Ellen, and I know all her tricks, and one of them is to pretend like she has something to do in the garden whenever she needs a minute away from the children inside. She comes out here for a little bit of peace and quiet before going back into her home and being inundated with drama again, and I guess that's just what some parents have to do to survive. But I've just disturbed her quiet time now, and by the time I have told her why, she's going to think that it would have been easier to stay indoors with her kids.

'So, I didn't take your advice,' I tell her as we take a seat on the patio steps that overlook her well-maintained garden. 'I got onto Paul's laptop.'

'How did you manage that?'

'I found his password in one of his old wallets,' I reply, although I'm still not sure it was an old wallet because he may have been using it alongside his other one. That's just one of the many things I need to figure out over the next few days.

'Wow, that's some good detective work. I'm glad you decided to take my advice on board.'

I laugh at my sister's sarcasm before shrugging my shoulders.

'I know you were just trying to help me get over things, but I really wanted to see what he had written to himself six months ago.'

'So did you?'

I nod my head, but my pensive expression must give away the fact that it isn't necessarily good news.

'What is it?' Ellen asks me.

'There were a couple of things in his message that didn't make sense.'

'Like what?'

'It's probably easier if I just show you.'

Reaching into my jeans pocket, I take out my mobile phone and open the email app before handing my device to my sister.

'I forwarded the email to myself,' I tell her as she starts to read it. 'This is what Paul wrote to himself six months ago.'

I wait patiently as Ellen reads the message and hear her say 'aww' at the part where Paul says that he wants our relationship to be stronger than ever, as well as chuckle, which I'm guessing is the bit where Paul mentions Chelsea being top of the league. But then she goes quiet again, and that's because she is now onto the parts of the message that aren't so heart-warming.

'On this day in six months, I will be feeling a lot better about my past. What does that mean?' Ellen asks me after she has finished reading the third thing that Paul wrote down.

'I have no idea. I'm hoping his parents might be able to help me with that one. But that's not the worst thing. Read the last one.'

I wait as Ellen does as she is told, and then I see her look up from the phone with an expression that can only be described as 'WTF'.

'Who the hell is Fiona?'

'I don't know.'

'Do you think he was seeing somebody else?'

'I'm not sure. But it doesn't sound good, does it?'

Ellen re-reads it again, but I've already tried that several times, and it doesn't help give any more answers. But I know what might, so it's time to mention it.

'I searched around on Paul's laptop for anybody called Fiona.'

'And what did you find?'

'A phone number.'

'Did you ring it?'

'No!'

'Why not?'

'I don't know. I'm too scared to.'

'Why?'

'Why do you think? In case Paul was cheating on me!'

'But wouldn't you want to know?'

'Of course, but I'm still scared.'

Ellen consults the message on my phone a couple more times before shaking her head and handing my device back to me.

'So, what do you think I should do?' I ask her as I put my phone back into my pocket. 'Should I call this Fiona and ask her how she knew Paul?'

'You could do,' Ellen replies, staring out across her neatly trimmed lawn. 'Or you could just delete the number, delete that message and move on with your life. Act like it doesn't exist. You don't need to know now that Paul is gone, I guess.'

'Really? That's your suggestion?'

'What do you want me to say?'

'I want you to tell me that I need to find out the truth.'

'I get why you would feel like you need to, but what good is it going to do now? Paul is dead. Maybe it's better to just hold onto the good memories you two had and take that forward into your next relationship when you feel ready to date again. If you go digging and find out some bad things, then you might never trust another man again.'

I stare at my sister to try and tell if she is being serious. Does she honestly think that I can just leave this and pretend like it never happened? I know I need to call Fiona, I just needed her to tell me it was the next logical step too. But she isn't telling me that. So now what should I do?

'I'm going to call her,' I say as I get up from the patio step and turn back to the house.

'I think that's a bad idea.'

'I have to know.'

'I think you're making a mistake.'

'Maybe.'

With that, I go back into the house, but I don't play with my nieces and be a good auntie. I just find a quiet room away from any noise.

And then I call Fiona.

13

It's my first day back at work since Paul died, and as expected, it's taken me a little while to get back up to speed. Working as a production assistant at a local television studio is a fun job but an extremely busy one, and I'm back sooner than expected because I needed the distraction. I could have taken another week on compassionate leave, but I decided to return to my role earlier because I needed a change from sitting around my house all day and thinking about Paul. But I also needed a distraction from thinking about the woman he may or may not have been having an affair with.

It's been three days since I first called Fiona to try and find out who she was and how she knew Paul, and my heart had been in my mouth as I had waited for her to pick up the phone. But she hadn't answered, nor had she answered any of the other fourteen calls I have made to her since. That might seem like an excessive number of times to ring somebody who obviously doesn't want to pick up, but it's not so bad when I have a good reason to be calling. Based on what Paul wrote in his message to himself six months ago, I need an explanation, and seeing as Paul is no longer around to give it to me, Fiona is the next best person to ask. But I have no idea why she isn't picking up, and because of that I still have no idea what was going on between them.

There's no way Fiona could recognise my number and know not to answer my calls, so either she no longer uses the phone, or she has just been very busy every time I rang and hasn't bothered to ring back yet. But I feel as though I can't stop trying because I'm not sure how else I could find out anything more.

'Have you got today's scripts? Please tell me you have them because we're already behind enough as it is.'

I turn around when I hear the question and see my director, Andy, looking at me with a harassed expression on his face. But he seemingly didn't know it was me he was talking to because when he sees me, his demeanour immediately changes.

'Sarah, I didn't realise it was you! What are you doing here? When did you get back?'

'Hey, Andy, I came back today.'

'Why? You shouldn't be here so soon after what happened! I thought the studio had given you time off.'

Andy looks as though he is about to go on the warpath with the HR department here before I let him know that it was my decision to return to work at this time.

'The studio has been great with me, but I just felt like I needed to come back and try and return to some normalcy again.'

'Are you sure?'

'Positive.'

Andy looks at me like he isn't sure if I'm being honest with him, but I nod my head to let him know to trust me. Maybe I am rushing things by being back at work so soon after losing Paul, but I have to come back here eventually, and there's not much keeping me occupied at home.

'I think Sally has the scripts,' I tell my director, pointing in the direction of my fellow production assistant, and Andy thanks me before scurrying away across the studio to chase my colleague up.

As I watch him go, I feel touched by his show of concern for me, but it's also a reminder that people are going to be treating me differently for a very long time. If things were normal, then Andy wouldn't have necessarily been so polite with me then. He would have just kept barking things at me until I gave him what he needed. That's not because he is a rude man but because he is a very stressed man with a demanding job. But it's not just Andy who is acting differently around me now. Everybody else. Family. Friends. Colleagues. All of them just want to know if I'm okay and keep looking at me with that sympathetic look in their eyes. It's a look that tells me that they feel sorry for me and have no idea how I am still able to be functioning relatively well after going through such a trauma. I'm sure there is also a little morbid curiosity in there too because they fear something bad like this happening in their own lives, and so they're interested in seeing how it affects another person. But I just want things to go back to being as normal as possible, and that means I want people to start telling me jokes again like they used to and not treating me as if I am some delicate object that needs handling with care.

I let out a deep sigh and prepare to head over to where some members of the cast and crew are assembled in preparation for the shooting of the next scene when I feel the vibration in my pocket.

Taking out my buzzing phone, I glance at the caller ID to make sure that it is a work-related call rather than a personal one or else I won't answer it now, but then I see the number, and my heart skips a beat.

It's Fiona.

She is calling me back.

I almost drop the phone in shock but manage to compose myself enough to keep hold of it and instead go behind one of the curtains at the back of the studio so that I am out of view of my employers. They might let me off taking a personal call considering what is going on in my life at this time, but I'd still rather they didn't see me because I don't want anybody to think that I'm taking liberties. But I'm out of view of everybody on the studio floor here, so I take a deep breath, and then I answer the call.

'Hello?'

'Hi, who is this?'

I pause because I'm not sure what the best way to answer that would be.

'Erm…' I say, filling the dead air over the call whilst trying to think of the right thing to say that won't just result in this woman hanging up on me immediately afterwards.

'I lost my phone at the weekend, but I've just got it back,' Fiona says, filling the dead air for me. 'I noticed I had rather a large number of calls from this number, so I'm just ringing to see who it is.'

‘Oh, okay,’ I mumble, processing the reasoning behind why she didn’t answer any of my fourteen calls over these last few days. ‘Thanks for calling back.’

‘Sorry, who is this?’ Fiona asks again, and I realise I’m not going to get away with asking her my question without answering hers first, so I just go for it.

‘My name is Sarah,’ I say, wondering if that will get any kind of a reaction from the other end of the line. But Fiona says nothing, so I add the next part to see what happens next.

‘I was Paul’s girlfriend before he died.’

I’m gripping the phone tightly as I hold it as close as possible to my ear so that I don’t miss a single part of Fiona’s answer when it comes. I’m expecting her to either pretend like she didn’t know Paul or perhaps take pity on me and ask me what I want to know. Everybody else has been taking pity on me lately, so she might as well join the club. But there is also a chance that she gives me a perfectly valid reason as to how she knew my boyfriend, and it could explain his cryptic message as well as put my fears to rest about him being unfaithful to me. Whatever happens, I’m about to get some answers.

And then I hear the line go dead.

14

I tried calling Fiona back after she hung up on me earlier, but perhaps unsurprisingly, she didn't answer. I'm not sure why I bothered trying to get through to her again however, because it's pretty obvious what her actions meant. She panicked as soon as she found out that I was Paul's girlfriend, and she ended the call as quickly as possible after that. It doesn't take a genius to work out what that means, and it isn't good.

The counsellor told me that taking things a day at a time would result in my situation getting easier for me, and that might have been the case if I had been left to grieve in normal circumstances. But finding out about the existence of Fiona and fearing that Paul was cheating on me has meant that every day has actually got harder instead of easier. I'm desperately searching for anything that will tell me that I've got my wires crossed and don't need to doubt the purity of the love that my boyfriend had for me, but such a thing has not been easy to find so far. Fiona could have put my mind at ease, but she only added fuel to the bonfire raging in my mind, and because of that I am unable to let things lie here.

I need to keep looking for more answers.

My search for answers has led me back to the place where I first stumbled across this unexpected mystery, and that is Paul's laptop. I'm sitting in front of it and using it to search for anything else that might shed some light on the man he really was. So far, I haven't found anything more to trouble me, just lots more photos of Paul with me when we were dating as well as a few older ones taken before we met. I know he spent some time travelling around Europe in his youth, as well as enjoying numerous nights out with his rowdy friends, who had all thankfully grown up more gracefully as the years had gone by. It's these photos that leave me feeling confused inside now because I no longer know how I should be viewing them. Should I look at Paul's smiling face with pride, or should I detest his happiness because was he really a good guy, or was he a liar? It's killing me not knowing because I'm not sure how to properly grieve and move on without the truth.

If it turns out that my beloved boyfriend was a cheat then I would find it much easier to move on because I would know that as much as I loved him, he wasn't perfect, and he didn't quite love me back in the same way. But what if I'm still wrong and he really was a good guy? I can't bear the thought of not mourning him properly if he really does deserve it.

Letting out a deep sigh before taking a sip of my hot coffee, I keep scrolling through his laptop, opening and closing files and waiting for something to catch my eye and reveal another potential layer of the man Paul really was.

And then I find something of interest.

It's a folder titled 'F'.

What does 'F' stand for?

Fiona?

But that's not the interesting part. What is interesting is that the folder doesn't open when I double-click it. Instead, I just get a small message bar pop up, which tells me that I have to enter a password if I want to get any further.

Why does Paul have a password-protected file on his personal computer? I could understand if he used this device a lot for work but he very rarely did, barring a few emails every now and again, so I doubt that's what could be hiding in this folder. So what could it be? I need to find out, and that's why I quickly pick up the scrap of paper with the password written on it that I used to access this laptop in the first place and try entering that.

But it doesn't work and neither does any of the other things I try.

Whatever this password is, it's stronger than his other ones.

'Damn it,' I say out loud to myself as I finish my coffee before getting up out of my seat and going into the kitchen to make another one. It's getting late, but I've all but made the decision to stop sleeping these days because it's no longer an easy thing for me to achieve, and besides, I have much more important things to do than lie in bed all night. I have detective work to do, and I'm going to get right back to it as soon as I have some more caffeine.

As I fix myself another drink, I think about the locked file on the laptop and how I might be able to open it and see the contents. I know my odds of finding another password written on a piece of paper amongst Paul's belongings are slim, though I am going to look, but I need to be prepared to take more decisive action. I might not possess the skills to get into that folder, but there will be people who do. There is a computer repair shop in town, and some of the clever guys in there might be able to help me or at least point me in the direction of somebody who can. I'm not sure what the rules are for helping somebody hack into a digital folder that doesn't belong to them because passwords exist for a reason, and that reason is for keeping people out. But I'm going to find out because as I finish making my coffee and head back into the dining room, I decide that I will take this laptop to the shop tomorrow.

But that's not going to be the only thing I do. I also want to pay Paul's parents a visit and talk to them to see if I can glean any insights into what the thing in Paul's past might be that caused him to mention it in his email to his future self. He wrote that he wanted to be feeling a lot better about his past in six months, and just like this situation with Fiona, I still don't understand what that means. I'm hoping that his mum and dad might have some ideas, and I pick up my phone to text them and ask them if it is okay if I call around at their place tomorrow to ask.

I haven't seen them for a couple of days now since the last time they called around to check that I was okay, and I have been expecting their visits to become more and more infrequent as time goes on. It must be pretty awkward for them both because while I was with Paul for a very long time, I wasn't married to him, so they might feel like they aren't sure how long they have to keep me in their lives. But they have still been texting me every day to see how I am, and I actually forgot to reply to their last message, so I'll answer that right now.

I tell them that I'm back at work (which is true) and feeling a little better (which is false) before mentioning that I would like to pay them a visit tomorrow. I don't expect them to say no and sure enough, they don't.

They respond to my message in less than two minutes, telling me that they are glad to hear that I am back at work again and are looking forward to seeing me tomorrow. With that done, I'm just about to put my phone down before I decide that I'm not finished with texting for the night. I want to send one more message, and it's probably one I should have sent a few days ago.

Texting Fiona, I ask her why she hung up on me and how she knew Paul. I'm not expecting a response, but it makes me feel a tiny bit better for trying, and you never know, she might have the courtesy to reply at some point. But unlike Paul's parents, she doesn't get back to me quickly, so I put my phone down and spend ten minutes trying unsuccessfully to guess the password on Paul's locked folder before giving up and taking my coffee upstairs to bed.

Coffee and sleep. Those things don't usually go together well.

But neither do love and infidelity either.

15

I expect that I don't look like the typical kind of customer to walk into this computer repair shop as I push open the door with Paul's laptop under my arm. I'm probably just being stereotypical, but as I came here today, I was expecting to see lots of people who were very different to me inside this place. Men with long hair and geeky t-shirts talking in all sorts of riddles and codes about I.T., the internet and that cool video game that just has to be played. I certainly didn't expect there to be too many women like me wandering around here amongst the aisles of laptops. What I know about technology could be condensed down onto half a sheet of A4 paper and relayed in about twenty seconds, so I'm very much out of my depth here. But to my surprise, the shop isn't full of nerdy men who look like they spend all their time in a dark room playing video games. There are just a couple of guys in suits standing at the counter talking to a couple of employees, one of which is female, and she doesn't look nerdy at all. She just looks like she could help me because she gives me a big smile when she sees me nervously walk in.

I've come here on my lunch break, that precious time when an employee can usually relax and switch off from their daily chores for an hour by eating sandwiches and gossiping with colleagues, to come and tick another job off my to-do list. I'm hoping that somebody in this shop is going to be able to help me access the mysterious locked file on my late boyfriend's computer, and as I make my way towards the counter where the customers and employees are gathered, I prepare to find out.

I take my place in line and wait patiently to be served, but I check my watch because I'm hoping that I'm not going to be here too long. I'm not sure I'll have the time, but I was going to try and really get the most out of my lunch break by calling in on Paul's parents too and asking them about his 'past', although I'm not sure that is the kind of conversation that could be squeezed into a small timeframe. Maybe I'll just have to go around to theirs after work tonight because I don't want them to feel like I'm rushing them. But I wouldn't mind if some of the employees in this shop felt like that.

The longer I stand here in the queue with the laptop under my arm, the more I begin to doubt what I'm trying to achieve. I have come here just presuming that somebody would be able to help me access the file that I don't know the password to, but that might not be the case. They might just shrug their shoulders and tell me they can't help me, and that would be a disappointment, and not just because I will have wasted my precious lunch hour. It will be because other than coming here, I have no idea how I am ever going to be able to access that folder and see if Paul had any more potential secrets to be unlocked.

'Hey! How's it going?'

I'm snapped out of my worrying by the friendly question from the woman behind the counter, and I take a few steps forward towards her now that the man who was being served in front of me has been seen to.

‘Hey! I was wondering if you could help me,’ I say as I place the laptop down on the counter in between us and open it up. ‘There’s a file on here that needs a password to open it, but I’ve forgotten what it is. Is there any way you can help me get into it?’

I’d already decided not to mention the fact that this laptop isn’t technically mine because that might make any employee here less keen to help me if they think I’m trying to access somebody else’s private property. I’m hoping they won’t have too many questions for me and instead, just give me some answers. But I’ve barely even got the laptop powered up before the woman on the other side of this counter lets me down.

‘I’m sorry, we aren’t able to help retrieve any passwords you might have had,’ she tells me with a simple shake of the head. ‘We mainly do repairs here.’

‘Oh, is there somewhere else that would be able to help?’

‘Well, to be honest, no, because I don’t know anywhere that allows people to hack into folders.’

‘I’m not trying to hack into it. I’ve just forgotten my password.’

‘That might be true, but not everybody has an innocent a reason as that. Some people want to get into folders that don’t belong to them, so can you imagine what would happen if people like me could help them do that? There would be no point anybody having a password anymore, would there?’

I guess that’s a good point, and it seems that my fears are being realised.

‘There must be some way that I can get into this folder. I mean, people must forget their passwords all the time, right? How do they manage to access files again?’

‘They don’t. If they’ve forgot the password then they can’t get in again.’

‘But I forget my password to my email account sometimes, and I just reset it!’

‘Yes, but that’s a lot different to a file. A person can prove that they own an email address, but they can’t prove that they own the contents of a particular file.’

I know I’m already wasting my time now, but I still insist on going to the file in question on the laptop and showing the woman so she can have a look for herself.

‘I just really need to access this folder. It’s for my job. It’s very important.’

The lies are just flowing from me now, and I can’t help but wonder if they used to do the same thing from Paul too. But it’s going to be hard to find out if I can’t crack this password.

‘I understand, but I’m sorry. I can’t help you. I suggest you write down your passwords somewhere and keep them safe in future, in case you forget again.’

The woman did seem pleasant enough when I first started talking to her, but I detect a slightly condescending tone to her voice now, and I guess she is starting to get tired of me now. I wonder how many times a day she gets somebody coming in here telling her that they have forgotten a password and asking her if she can help them, as if all those years of studying I.T. and being around modern equipment was done just so a forgetful person could use her to retrieve something that had slipped their mind.

I could stand here for another few minutes pleading my case, but that would be a waste of this woman's time, as well as a waste of what is now remaining of my lunch hour. That's why I reluctantly close down the laptop and pick it up from the counter before smiling weakly and turning to leave.

'If you have any other issues with your laptop then don't hesitate to come back!' the woman behind the counter calls after me as I head for the door, but I'm not expecting to ever come back here again. I could try another computer shop, but I guess I will just get told the same thing. I suppose it's comforting to know that people can't just go around asking I.T. experts to hack people's passwords, but it's not much help for me and my problem right here. But what can I do? I guess this is a dead end.

I leave the shop and step back out onto the bright and breezy high street before turning left and heading in the direction of where my car is parked. I paid for a full hour at the car park because that was the only option the parking meter gave me, but I've barely been gone fifteen minutes. Never mind, at least I guess I have time to call in on Paul's parents before going back to work. At least I think I do until I hear the shouting behind me and turn around to see who is trying to get my attention.

'Excuse me! Hey, lady!'

I see the young man making all the noise and also realise that he is talking to me because he is looking right at me as he hurries up the street in my direction. I notice that he is wearing the same kind of t-shirt that the woman I just spoke to in the computer shop was wearing, so I guess he works in that shop too. But I don't know why he could be running after me unless I left something behind and he's trying to return it to me. But I don't think that I did.

'Hey!' the young man says as he reaches me, and despite it only being a short distance from the shop to where I stand on the pavement, he seems surprisingly out of breath. Then again, he is overweight. He also looks to be around eighteen, and with his greasy hair and his nervous disposition, he fits the bill of the kind of men I was expecting to see when I first entered that computer shop a little earlier.

'Is everything okay?' I ask him as he gets his breath back and tucks away a strand of dark, scraggly hair from his forehead.

'I work in the computer shop,' he tells me, and that's when I see the name badge attached to his t-shirt that says 'Calvin.'

'Oh, okay,' I reply, not really sure where he is going with this. Unless…

Oh, God, is he going to ask me on a date?

'I heard your problem, and I think I can help you,' he tells me, and it takes me a few seconds to figure out what he means.

'With my password?'

'Yeah, I know how you can get into the file without it.'

'You do? But the woman in the shop said it couldn't be done.'

'It can be done.'

'Oh, right. Okay. Shall I come back to the shop?'

'No. I'll have to come to you.'

'I'm sorry?'

'Your house. I'll have to come to your house if you want me to open the file for you.'

'Why can't we just go back to the shop?'

The young man hesitates a moment, and that's when I realise what he means when he says he can help me.

'You're not supposed to be doing this, are you?'

'Not really. But I can help you, if you want? It won't cost too much either.'

'How much?'

'Five hundred.'

I laugh at the price I have just been quoted. But the teenager in front of me doesn't seem bothered. He just keeps looking over his shoulder in the direction of the shop, presumably worried that his manager is going to come out and see what he is up to.

'That's a lot of money.'

'But you need to open the file, right? Well, I can do it for you. I have the equipment you need, and it won't take too long.'

I should tell this guy that I'm not interested in partaking any further in some dodgy deal. I mean, is what he is proposing illegal? I should ask. But then I think about how desperate I am to know if Paul was being honest with me or if there was another side to him.

The locked folder on his laptop. The cryptic message in his six-month email. And Fiona.

I need to know what is going on.

That is why I accept this young man's offer to help me, and he types my address in his phone before telling me that he can't come around to mine tonight because he has to go to night college, but he will be around tomorrow evening if that's okay. I tell him that it will be, and then he reminds me of the price we have agreed on. Then he scurries away back to the shop, and I watch him go inside before getting on my way again. But I'm not headed to the car park now.

I'm going to the cash machine.

16

My afternoon at work went quickly, although it was hard to concentrate on my tasks at the studio after what had happened on my lunch break. Agreeing to give a large sum of money to a dodgy teenager who works in a computer shop might not be the most traditional of ways to spend a lunch hour, but I did it, and despite my worries, I am hoping it means I am one step closer to opening that file on Paul's laptop and finding out if he was hiding anything else from me. I really hope there is something worthwhile in there because otherwise, I would have wasted £500, but then again, if the folder contains nothing but innocent things then it might mean

Paul was a good guy, and I might be worrying about nothing.

I guess all will be revealed when Calvin pays me a visit tomorrow night.

But I'm not going to waste this evening waiting for the next one, and that's why I'm walking up to the front door of Paul's parents' house now and preparing to knock on it. It's time to find out if there is anything in my late boyfriend's past that I needed to know about sooner.

The door is answered quickly after I knocked, and I suspect that Paul's parents were loitering near the door because they would have been expecting me. It's Paul's father who I see first, a tall, wiry man wearing glasses that I've never seen him wear and an expression that tells me things have been difficult for him recently.

'Hi, John,' I say as I force a smile onto my face, which seems like a weird thing to do in front of a man who is grieving the loss of his son. But I don't want the mood to be too heavy between us tonight, for all our sakes.

'Hi, Sarah,' he says as he allows me inside before giving me a slightly awkward hug, and I feel his shoulder blades through his shirt as we embrace.

'How are you doing?' I ask him as he closes the front door, and he just gives me a shrug before nodding towards an internal door in the house and looking very glum about things.

'I'm okay. It's more Ruth that I'm worried about.'

That doesn't sound good, and I follow John into the living room where I see the television set is on and being watched by Paul's mum, although the vacant look behind her eyes suggests she isn't paying attention to anything that is happening on the screen.

'Sarah is here,' John tells his wife before picking up the remote control from the armchair and turning the volume down on the TV, so conversation will be easier. But I think we're going to need more than a quiet room to make this conversation easier.

'Hi Ruth,' I say as I stand awkwardly on the edges of the room, looking nervously at the older woman on the sofa and wondering if she is even going to be up to having a visitor this evening.

I know that she looked devastated at the funeral, but she looks even more withdrawn now like she hasn't eaten since and maybe she hasn't. But unlike John, who has always been skinny, Ruth used to be plump and full-faced. Unfortunately, since the loss of her son, she now looks gaunt and haggard. But I could say the same about myself.

'Sarah. It's nice to see you,' she says, and she goes to get up to give me a hug, but I tell her not to worry and instead go over to her, taking a seat beside her and hugging her where she sits.

She holds onto me tightly as we embrace and we hold it for a few more seconds than a person normally would do when they hug someone else, but I can tell that she needs the human contact, and I guess I need it too because I keep squeezing back just as much.

John offers me a cup of tea and then disappears into the kitchen to make it as I take off my coat and spend a few minutes asking Ruth how she has been. It's a difficult conversation to have, and both of us let the other one know that we haven't been sleeping much, or eating much, or doing much of anything other than thinking about Paul. But I suppose there is one difference between us and it's how we have been thinking about Paul. Ruth has been mourning her son, reminiscing on all the happy memories while cursing life for being denied the chance to make any more, and while I had started off by doing the same, I'm now thinking about Paul in other ways. I'm wondering if he might not have been as perfect as the man Ruth thinks he was.

I wait until John has returned with the cups of tea and taken a seat in his armchair before I decide to gently broach the subject of Paul and his past.

'There's something I need to ask you, and I'm not sure if you can help, but maybe you can,' I begin, watching John take a sip of his tea while Ruth completely ignores hers as it sits on the coffee table in front of her. 'Six months ago, Paul and I did this thing where we wrote down something we wanted to be happening in our lives half a year later.'

I see John look a little confused about what I've just said, but I can't be bothered to explain all the ins and outs of 'writing your future', so I just push on.

'One of the things that Paul wrote was that he hoped he would feel a lot better about his past. I've been trying to figure out what that means. Do you have any idea?'

'His past?' John repeats back to me before having a good think about it, and I wait with hope that he might be able to come to some sort of a conclusion. But he doesn't.

'I'm sorry, I have no idea what he could have meant there,' the father tells me with a shrug of his bony shoulders.

'How about you, Ruth?' I ask the woman beside me. 'Do you have any idea?'

But Ruth is staring at the TV even though the volume is too low to hear what is being said on it, and I'm not even convinced that she heard what I just asked her.

'Ruth?' I try again, and she suddenly turns to me, looking surprised as if she had forgotten I was even here.

'Sorry?'

'I was just asking if anything had happened in Paul's past that might have been troubling him more recently. Is there anything you knew of?'

'Like what?'

'I don't know. Any trauma? Bad memories? Anything?'

'No, nothing like that.'

'Was he bullied? Or ever do anything he shouldn't have done?'

'No. He was a good boy.'

I realise that I'm not getting anywhere fast here and wonder if I should just leave it.

‘Was there anything else Paul did or said that hinted at something that had been troubling him?’ John asks me.

‘No, nothing. Just what he wrote in that message to himself.’

‘Perhaps it was just something to write then. Maybe there wasn’t anything in his past. I’m sure we would have known about it if there was.’

John’s right. Between the three of us, we knew Paul long enough to know if there had been any events that might have caused him to be worrying about them in the months before he passed. It’s not a satisfactory answer to my question, but I realise that there’s not much else I can do, at least not here anyway. Perhaps there will be something of interest in the locked folder on his laptop that Calvin is going to apparently unlock for me tomorrow. But for now, I can’t do much more, other than bother Ruth and John, who both look as though me pestering them with questions about their dead son is the last thing they need to get over his death.

I finish my tea quickly and tell the couple that I better get going because I have an early start in the morning, so John tells me that he will show me out. Ruth stays where she is on the sofa as I say goodbye to her, and I notice that she still hasn’t touched her cup of tea as I go. There’s no doubt she has taken Paul’s death the worst out of the three of us. At least John and I are still functioning. Ruth looks like a shell of the woman she used to be, and it’s so unfair to see her like this.

As I say goodbye to John and walk away down the dark driveway back to where my car is parked on this quiet residential street, my heart aches for the couple I am leaving behind but not just because they are suffering the loss of their son. It's also because they have been robbed of so many good times, just like I have, not least of which would have been the wedding day when I would have eventually married Paul. Ruth would have lapped up the opportunity to put on a glamorous outfit for the occasion, and I'm sure that John would have enjoyed wearing a nice suit too, as well as attending whatever stag do Paul had organised ahead of the big day. But now they are just two sad people sitting in their home with only photos to look back on, and it is little wonder why Ruth can't even bring herself to take a sip of tea. What's the point? It won't bring Paul back.

As I reach my car, I wonder if there is any point in me trying to find out what Paul meant in his message and if he really was seeing some woman called Fiona behind my back. He's gone, so he isn't here to answer for himself, and there won't be any comfort to be found for me either. I'll still be alone whatever I do. Should I just save myself £500 and cancel Calvin tomorrow, leaving that file on Paul's laptop locked forever?

That's what I spend the whole drive home thinking about.

But by the time I get back to my house and walk into my dark, empty abode, I realise that I have very little else in my life to keep me occupied. Other than work, I have nothing. This investigation into Fiona and the laptop has given me a purpose. I might as well spend that £500. It's not as if I'm going to spend it on clothes or shoes for a big night out or a holiday anytime soon.

That’s it decided then.
I’ll see Calvin tomorrow.
And then I will see what is in that locked folder.

17

Calvin arrived at my home twenty minutes later than he said he would do tonight, and he looked nervous as he stepped through my front door with a backpack on his shoulders as he apologised and told me how he had got lost. I close the door behind him while hoping that his I.T. skills are going to be better than his navigation ones before taking him into the dining room, where Paul's laptop is already on the table, ready to be used.

I feel strange offering a drink to a teenager who has come here to help me hack a computer file, whilst also charging me £500 for the privilege of doing so, but I ask anyway because I'm a good host, and Calvin tells me that he would like a can of Cola if I have one. I don't, so he has to make do with a glass of lemonade, but he seems happy enough as he removes the backpack from his shoulder and starts unzipping it.

By the time I have returned to the dining room with his drink, Calvin has laid out all sorts of fancy equipment on the table, and he is currently connecting some of it to the laptop, making me wonder just how much effort it is really going to take to crack this password. But before he gets to work, and just after he has taken a sip of his lemonade, Calvin very shyly broaches the subject of his payment.

'Oh, of course,' I say, reaching into my jeans pocket and taking out the envelope that is stuffed full of twenty-pound notes, coming to a total value of £500.

As I hand the envelope to the teenager, I realise that he could very easily just do a runner with the money now and not give me what I have paid for, but he doesn't do that. He doesn't even count the money. He just puts the envelope into his backpack and then sits down in front of the laptop ready to start work, and I feel slightly touched that he trusts me enough not to check his payment before proceeding.

'Is this the folder here?' he asks me, pointing to the yellow icon on the laptop screen.

'Yeah,' I reply, watching him as he double-clicks it and gets confirmation that he does need a password to proceed past this point.

'Okay, cool,' he says, which is what every person his age seems to say about everything, before he fiddles around with some of the cables that are linked to the equipment that he brought here to help him this evening.

'Is this illegal?

Calvin looks up at me and probably thinks the same thing as I am, which is that it is a little late to be asking that question now.

'Never mind, I don't want to know,' I tell him, batting my hand in the air as if it's no big deal if I could go to prison for this.

Calvin laughs a little nervously before turning back to the laptop and carrying on with what he was doing before I interrupted him.

'How long will this take?' I ask him as I see a new toolbar open on the screen.

'It's always different, but it shouldn't be more than ten minutes.'

'Wow, ten minutes?'

'It could be quicker, but I don't have the best kit on the market to do it that fast. I just need to download some software into your device, and then I will be able to do anything on it.'

'Still, five hundred pounds is a lot for ten minutes' work, isn't it?'

'You wouldn't be saying that if you knew how much all of this cost,' Calvin replies, and he gestures to all the equipment around him, which shuts me up because I don't have a clue what any of it costs, but it must be expensive.

I decide that it might be best if I don't talk to Calvin again until he has finished what he is doing, so I just take a seat at the other end of the dining table and wait for him to tell me when he is done. I watch his fingers typing away on the keyboard over the next few minutes, as well as his eyes darting around the screen as he concentrates and, in the end, the timeframe he gave to me flies by.

'All done!' he says as he sits back in his seat with a satisfied grin on his face.

'That's it? The file's unlocked?' I ask him as I get out of my seat and go over to the laptop to see what he can see on the screen.

'Yep. You're in.'

'Great, thanks.'

I look at the laptop screen and see several more files now, which all look like the one Calvin has just opened, and for a second, I fear that I've just unlocked one folder only to be met by several more locked ones.

'Don't worry, you can access all of them. The password was only on the master file,' Calvin assures me, and that's a relief because I didn't fancy going back to the cash machine to withdraw any more money to give to this kid.

'Okay,' I say as I lean in and stare at the screen, but I guess I won't learn much more until I start clicking on these other files, and I don't really want to do that with Calvin here with me because I'm not sure what I will find.

'Do you want me to help with anything else?' the teenage I.T. specialist asks me, but I tell him that will be all, and he looks a little disappointed before starting to unplug his equipment and put it into his bag.

I impatiently wait for him to get all his things together and finish his drink before I lead him to the front door and prepare to bid him farewell. But before I can, he asks me a surprising question.

'Would you like to go for a drink sometime?'

'Excuse me?'

'Do you want to go for a drink with me?'

'Like a date?'

'It could be.'

I don't know whether to laugh or be shocked by this young man's confidence, but either way, I'm not going to say yes.

'That's very sweet. But I think you're a bit too young for me,' I tell him as I open the door and step aside so that he can leave.

'I'm eighteen,' he protests. 'And you're not that old!'

'Charming, but I think I'll pass, thank you.'

'Don't worry, the drinks will be on me,' he tries, clearly not one for giving up easily. But I guess that's an easy offer for him to make, considering I have just given him an envelope full of cash.

'Again, that's very sweet. But I'll have to say no.'

'Why? Do you have a boyfriend?'

The question catches me off guard, and the word boyfriend hits me like a punch to the stomach. I always used to say yes to that question on the rare occasions that a guy was trying to pick me up in a bar or at work, but now I guess I can't say that anymore. I am single, even though I didn't choose to be. But that doesn't mean I'm still going to go on a date with an eighteen-year-old, especially one who I just paid to do something that the police might be interested in knowing about.

'It's time for you to go. Thanks for your help, and please don't tell anybody about this.'

'Okay,' Calvin mutters as he begrudgingly leaves without a hot date to look forward to, and I watch the teen shuffle his way up my driveway before disappearing down the dark street with his shoulders hunched and his greasy head bowed low.

I smile to myself as I close the door because it's good to know that I have still 'got it,' or at least I have as far as attracting somebody half my age who is definitely not boyfriend material, before I go back into the dining room and look at the laptop.

It's time to sit down and start looking through this folder that Calvin just unlocked for me.

There's nothing else between me and whatever the contents happen to be.

So why do I feel as if I'm too scared to start looking? Why do I feel as if I need a strong drink to hand before I do? I don't know, but either way, I spend a few minutes in the kitchen pouring myself a large glass of wine first before I finally take my seat in front of the laptop and put my finger onto the mousepad.

I move the cursor across the screen until it is over the first file before pausing.

Then I take a sip of my wine, followed by a deep breath.

And then I double-click to open it.

18

The first file was a photo of another woman. The second and third files were photos of the same woman, only this time Paul was with her too. They were both smiling and looking very happy together as if they were a couple in love. I can only assume that they were, but the problem is that Paul does not look young in these photos as if this is a person he dated before he met me. He looks just like he did when I was in a relationship with him, which can only mean one thing.

He was having an affair.

And I assume this woman in the pictures is Fiona.

I absent-mindedly continue clicking through the rest of the files, but I'm barely processing the images that flash up on the laptop screen now. Just more and more photos of Paul and this woman. In bars. In restaurants. On a boat on a lake somewhere. Lots of fun adventures together, and all while I was presumably sitting at home thinking about what a wonderful boyfriend I had. I don't know why I'm torturing myself by continuing to look, but I go through every single file until I have seen every single photograph, and now I guess there is no doubt in my mind about what Paul meant in his message to himself six months ago. He was cheating on me, and while his message made it sound like he was feeling guilty and wanted to end his illicit relationship, it still doesn't make up for the fact that he was lying to me when he was alive.

Having reached the last file and having no more to open, I stare at the photo on the screen, which is yet another one of my late boyfriend looking very happy with a woman who isn't me. I keep looking at the image until it goes blurry, and that's because my eyes have filled with tears, and I can now no longer see properly.

I wipe my bloodshot eyes with the sleeve of my sweater, whilst finishing my glass of wine and thinking about going to pour myself another one. But my instincts take over, and I decide that I have a better use for the glass in my hand.

I throw it as hard as I can at the wall in front of me, and it shatters loudly, sending tiny shards of glass in every direction and ensuring that it won't be safe to walk through this room in bare feet for a very long time. But I don't care about what I have just done, and I would do it again if I had another glass to hand. I feel like I want to keep smashing things, and I look around the room at all the other objects I could destroy, but I'm simply too drained to get out of my seat and go over to any of them. I suppose that is a good thing, or I would surely break every single thing in here and leave this part of the house looking like a warzone. As it is, I just remain in my seat at the dining table and think about how this is the same table where Paul and I used to have so many romantic meals together.

Candles. Wine. Music. I used to love our date nights at home when I would cook up something tasty while Paul would set the table and make sure the ambience in the dining room was perfect for two young lovers who wanted to enjoy each other's company. Now this same table has become the setting for the place where I have discovered all of my boyfriend's lies, and tonight has wiped out ten years of happy memories.

I suppose I should hate the woman in the photos, but I find myself hating Paul more. He's the one who lied to me, not her. I wonder if this woman even knew I existed, or did Paul lie to her too? I think back to when Fiona hung up on me the other day, and that would suggest that she knew who I was, but is this woman on screen even her, or is it somebody else? How many women was Paul seeing at the same time as me?

I realise that just knowing I have been betrayed isn't enough. I need to know more details like when it began and how long it went on. That's why I need to find out who this woman in the photos is. It might be Fiona, but I only have her phone number, and it's not much use to me if she is just going to keep hanging up. I need to find her in person and speak to her. Only then will I really learn the extent of what Paul was up to.

But how do I do that? How can I find this woman in the pictures? Hire a private detective? Even if that was going to work, it wouldn't be cheap, and I'm not made of money, and certainly not after I just gave £500 to Calvin. There has to be another way. A way that I can do it myself. A cheaper way. A faster way.

And then I have an idea.

Taking my mobile phone from my pocket, I open up the first of several social media apps that I have downloaded on my device and type in the name 'Fiona'. I know it will return results for people in my area first, and I assume Fiona is nearby if Paul was seeing her.

Then all I will have to do is look through the results and see if I recognise the same woman as the one in the photos on this laptop.

It's a long shot, but it's all I've got, and at least I will only lose time doing it and not money.

The app tells me that there are several people in my area going by the name Fiona, but I suppose it's better to get lots of results than too few, so I start clicking on each of them to look at the photo in their profiles. These are Fionas of different ages and hair colours, but I quickly skip past anybody who doesn't match the appearance of the woman in the photos on Paul's laptop.

It's long and tedious, and I knew this was a very unlikely way of producing the result I wanted, but just as I am close to giving up, I see her.

The woman in the pictures with Paul. Her image is staring back at me now from my mobile phone. I have found her. Her name is Fiona Hill. A quick check on the rest of her photos confirms that this is definitely the same woman that I have been looking for.

Moving on from the pictures, I read through her bio to learn more about her, and that's when I see that her relationship status is listed as single. I almost scoff at that because from what I have seen, she was as far from single as could be. How many photos does it take with your arm draped around another man before you are considered to be in a relationship? But I assumed she listed herself as single because she knew exactly who Paul was and knew that she couldn't be in an official relationship with him because he was already seeing somebody else.

My teeth are grinding together as I continue to read Fiona's bio in which she tells anybody who reads it that she is a lover of travel, fiction books and cooking, as well as stating that she 'longs for adventure' and 'lives for today.' That's certainly one way of saying that she likes to get involved with unavailable men.

But it's the last part of her bio that gets my attention the most, and when I read it, I almost drop my phone because I can't quite believe how easy it will be to find her now.

She has stated her place of work, and all I have to do is click on the name of the company, and the next webpage to load is the one that will give me its address.

I know where Fiona will be tomorrow.

She will be at the address on my screen right now.

I guess that's now where I'm going to be too.

19

I have the proverbial butterflies in my stomach as I walk through the glass doors that lead into this office in the middle of town and make my way over to the receptionist behind the desk. I have already captured her attention before I have even said a word, and I'm guessing that is because I'm not dressed like the other people who visit this office every day. Instead of wearing a blouse, skirt and heels like many other women would who work in a place like this, I'm wearing a hoody, jeans and trainers. I'm not scruffy, I'm just wearing the clothes that I can wear in my workplace. But a television studio has a much more casual dress code than an office, and I'm starting to regret not trying to blend in more as I reach the desk and see the receptionist looking me up and down.

'Can I help you?' she asks me, perhaps wondering if I've just wandered in off the street to ask her if she can spare some change.

'Yes, I'm hoping you can,' I reply with false confidence. 'I'm hoping to speak with Fiona Hill. Is she here?'

'Do you have an appointment?'

'Er, no, I don't.'

'I'll have to check if she is available.'

'Thank you.'

I face an anxious wait as the receptionist picks up her phone and dials the four-digit number that must be connecting her to Fiona's desk somewhere else in this building. I attract a few more puzzled glances from some of the other employees here who pass through reception while I wait, men in their shirts and ties wondering why I look so scruffy, and women in smart suits probably feeling sorry for the fact that I don't look anywhere near as powerful as them. I wonder what Fiona will be wearing when I finally meet her.

I wonder how much better she will look than I do.

I don't even know what her job title is here, only that this is where she comes to work, so I could have just asked for the manager of this company for all I know. But then the receptionist starts talking, and I'm guessing Fiona isn't quite as high up in this organisation as I might fear.

'Hey, Fiona. It's Kelsey. I've got a lady here in reception asking to speak with you.'

I watch as the receptionist listens down the phone before she looks up at me again and asks me for my name.

'Erm…'I say, hesitating because I fear that being honest and giving it will not be the best way to get Fiona to come and speak to me. She couldn't hang up the phone quick enough the last time I tried getting in touch, so imagine what she would do if she found out I was in the same building as her.

She might jump out of a window.

Kelsey stares at me as if I'm some idiot who can't even remember their own name, and I realise I just need to give a name, any name, so I tell her that I'm called Amy and hope that's enough. I don't know where

I got Amy from, but it was the first name that popped into my head.

Kelsey passes on the name to Fiona before coming back with another question a few seconds later.

'Sorry, Fiona wants to know what this is about?'

Damn it. I need another lie.

'I just really need to speak to her if she could just give me two minutes.'

I hope that will be enough to convince Fiona to get up from her desk and come to reception, but I don't know and can only cross my fingers as Kelsey passes on my message.

But then the receptionist hangs up the phone and tells me to take a seat, and I guess that is good news, so I do as I am told before anybody can change their mind and tell me to leave.

Sinking down into one of several plush leather chairs dotted around this reception area, I do my best to stay calm as I wait for the door behind Kelsey to open and Fiona to walk out and see me. I'm not sure if she will recognise me as Paul's partner, but I hope not because if she does, then I expect she will look to make a hasty exit. That remains to be seen, but until I see her, all I can do is jiggle my legs up and down nervously and fidget with my hands.

A few minutes go by, and Fiona still hasn't appeared, and I'm starting to worry that she has somehow been tipped off that there is a jilted lover in reception and that she shouldn't go down there to face the music. But that is silly because there is nobody here to tip her off. She must just be busy and have things to finish before she can come and see me. I'm not sure what could be more important than what I am here to talk about, but I try not to get annoyed and remind myself that I don't want to frighten this woman off before I have had a chance to ask her my questions and get some answers.

The door behind Kelsey suddenly swings open, and I brace myself for an awkward interaction with the woman coming out of it, but it's a false alarm. It's not Fiona, just one of her colleagues, so I ease myself back into the seat and take a deep breath. My heart is hammering away in my chest, and my hands are clammy as if I'm here for a job interview rather than a personal matter. I wish it was an interview that brought me here because that would be easier than what I have really come here to do.

And then I see her.

She pushes open the door behind her colleague just before it closes and she walks right into reception, looking towards Kelsey and asking where her visitor is. Then Kelsey points at me, and I watch Fiona closely for her reaction.

I see her eyes widen. I see her smile vanish.

And then I see her turn back to the door she just came out of.

'Wait!' I cry as I get up from my seat and rush towards her, realising now that she does know who I am on appearance alone and is trying to escape before I can confront her.

Fiona is halfway through the door back into the office, but I reach her quickly and plead with her to speak with me. Kelsey jumps out of her seat and looks as if she is trying to figure out if she needs to call security, or worse, the police, but I can't focus on her. I need to get Fiona to stop because if she goes through this door and it closes behind her, then I won't be able to get to her again.

'Please, I just want some answers! You owe me that!' I cry in the direction of Fiona's back because she is still heading away from me.

But that plea gets her to turn around, and she looks at me standing before her, no doubt looking sad, desperate and lonely.

'You know who I am, don't you?' I ask her, and she nods her head slowly. 'Then you know why I am here. Please. I'm not mad at you. I just want to talk.'

'Is everything okay?' Kelsey asks Fiona with her hand on the phone as if she is ready to make an emergency call if required, but thankfully, Fiona nods her head and tells the receptionist that everything is fine. Then she asks her colleague if any of the meeting rooms are free, and Kelsey tells her that Meeting Room One is available for the next ten minutes.

'That will be enough time,' Fiona says before looking back to me and pushing the door back open to invite me in.

Then she tells me to follow her, and I don't need telling twice.

Finally, I'm about to learn the truth about Paul and this other woman.

20

I stare at the woman sitting across the table from me in this expansive meeting room, and I wait for her to speak first. I want to know what the first words out of her mouth will be. An apology? That would be nice. An excuse for her behaviour? There is no excuse, but I'd be happy for her to try and come up with one before I shoot it down. Or maybe a denial of her guilt and a transfer of all the blame onto Paul, which would be very convenient for her because Paul is no longer around to give his side of the story. Whatever Fiona is going to come up with in this room right here, it better be good.

'How did you find out?' she asks me as her eyes try and hold mine, but she gives up quickly and ends up looking down at the table most of the time instead.

'It's a long story. But it's true? You were having an affair with him?'

I watch as Fiona nods, and even though it's a brutal confirmation of what I feared, it also feels like a weight off my shoulders. I haven't been acting like a mad woman recently. I've been on the right track all along.

'When did it start?' I ask.

'Four years ago.'

I feel as if all the air has been sucked out of the room as Fiona gives me her answer. Four years? Paul was betraying me for that long? How could he do it? This wasn't just some one-night thing when he got drunk and made a mistake. It was four whole years of his life with me, and even though the photos on his laptop told me it was more serious than a short fling, it's still shocking to learn the extent of it.

'How did it start?'

'I met him on a night out. We got chatting at the bar. He was drunk, but so was I. We ended up giving each other our numbers, and then we started messaging after that.'

'When did you find out he had a long-term girlfriend?'

Fiona looks hesitant to answer that one, but I glare at her to let her know that she is going to have to.

'About three months in.'

'Wow, you knew about me almost the whole time, and you didn't think to ever stop?'

'I'm sorry. But I didn't know you. You were just a name. I know it was wrong, but I liked him.'

'I loved him!'

Fiona nods her head at that, not daring to argue with me about strength of feelings because it's plainly obvious that I have her beat there.

'How did you find out about me?' I ask as my clammy hands are clasped together tightly in my lap.

'Paul told me. I had no idea he was seeing somebody else until then.'

'He volunteered that information?'

'Yeah, he just told me.'

At first, I can't think of a reason why Paul would start having an affair and then confess to his mistress that he was already seeing somebody else, but then I think about it, and I realise why.

'He cared about you,' I say, shaking my head.

'We were close,' Fiona tells me with her eyes now lowered all the time. 'I loved him, and I think he loved me.'

'I thought that too once,' I say to let Fiona know that Paul had us both fooled.

'Look, I'm sorry about this, but I'm not sure what you have come here to do. I know what we were doing was wrong, but really, it was Paul that was most at fault.'

'That's nice of you to put it on him.'

'I didn't mean it like that. I heard the news. I know what happened with him with that accident. I'm just saying that he lied to us both, and we both fell for it. He told me he was going to leave you one day, and I believed him. If he hadn't said that then maybe I would have ended it myself.'

Every fibre in my being is screaming at me to reach across the table and pull this woman by the hair towards me because I know it will make me feel better for at least two seconds before I let go. But I restrain from physical violence because as horrible as this is, I know Fiona is right. This is Paul's fault. Not hers. Not mine. *His.*

'He was thinking of leaving you,' I tell Fiona after a quiet moment has passed between us.

'How do you know?'

'He wrote it down. Said he was going to end things with you within six months.'

'So that's how you found out?'

'That's what tipped me off. Then I found the photos of you two on his laptop, and I guess it was obvious then.'

'I suppose he had been feeling guilty about what he was doing.'

'Maybe. Who knows? I thought I knew him better than anyone, but now I see that I never knew him at all.'

I stare at Fiona for a few seconds, but she still doesn't look up at me, and I guess I've got as much out of this interaction as I need.

'What are you going to do?' she asks me solemnly.

'What can I do? Just go home and get on with my life.'

'Do you still miss him?'

'What does that have to do with anything?'

'I'm just asking. I still miss him. Even though I know he wasn't perfect. I still miss him anyway.'

I feel like telling Fiona that she has no right to miss the man I loved, but now I have calmed down a little, I can see that she is hurting almost as much as I am.

Almost.

'Was there anybody else?' I ask her before I stand up and leave this depressingly clinical meeting room.

'What do you mean?'

'Did Paul ever mention any other women?'

'No, definitely not!'

'But there could have been more?'

'I don't know. Maybe. But I doubt it.'

'Why? What makes you doubt it?'

'He didn't seem like the kind of guy to make a habit of it.'

I laugh at that remark.

'He didn't seem like the kind of guy to do something like this once, never mind multiple times,' I tell Fiona with a shake of the head, and with that, I'm ready to get out of here.

'I'm sorry,' Fiona tells me again as I head for the door, but I leave without saying another word, walking out of the room and back through reception, ignoring Kelsey as I go until I am on the other side of the glass entrance doors, back in the fresh air on the street outside.

I take several deep breaths as I walk away from the office, the same office that I was eager to go into but now am more eager to get away from. Fiona was open and honest with me, at least she was after she tried to run away from me anyway. I appreciate the fact that she has told me the truth, even though I don't care for that truth one bit. But now I know for sure what Paul was up to behind my back, I guess it will make getting over him a little easier. It was horrible mourning a man who I thought adored me more than anything in the world, so it shouldn't be as awful to mourn a man who didn't care for me as much as I cared for him.

I reach my parked car and automatically start driving in the direction of home, but I need to vent to somebody, so I change course and go to my sister's house instead. I don't even know if she will be in, but I'll just sit outside and wait for her to come home if not. I'd rather do that than spend the rest of today sitting in my empty house with that damn laptop. I never know, I might get lucky and find Ellen is home, and we can open a bottle of wine before I tell her all about the crazy stuff that I have found out ever since I ignored her advice and started snooping into Paul's private life. There is no doubt she will be shocked to hear what he was up to, as well as what I got up to in order to uncover it. But it will feel good to get it off my chest, and then I can ask her for her advice on what I do next.

I'm pretty sure I know what she will say. She will tell me to throw out all of Paul's things as soon as possible and try and forget all about him.

This time, I think I will take her advice.

21

Being around my sister and her family for the last few hours has been just what I needed to remind myself that not everything is messed up in my world. It's hard to feel too bad when you receive the love of a sibling, never mind two young nieces who are incredibly cute and incredibly funny. Since arriving here from the office where I got the harsh truths from Fiona, I have spent some time drawing with Molly, playing dolls with Bethany and listening to Ellen tell me all about the gossip in her workplace. It's been just what I needed to give my mind a rest from all the stresses and strains I have been under lately, and as it gets later in the evening, I feel ready to really open up to my sister about what has been going on with me since I last saw her.

I haven't told her everything yet because I didn't want to say anything in front of the girls or Alex, Ellen's husband. But now the kids have been put to bed, and Alex has just told us that he is going to go to the gym, so that leaves the pair of us alone to really have a heart-to-heart.

I receive a second glass of wine from my sister before she sinks into the sofa beside me, and after hearing the front door close behind Alex, I now feel ready to unload.

I tell Ellen everything, from the photos on the laptop, which I was able to see after paying a teenage I.T. expert to access them for me, as well as tracking down Fiona on social media, and finally, to the confrontation we had at her workplace. I tell her how I know for sure now that Paul was cheating on me, and it was a serious affair, not just some fling. Then I end by telling my sister that I feel as if the last decade of my life has been a waste and that I feel like I want to get revenge on Paul for what he has done to me. But therein lies my problem.

'How do you get revenge on a dead guy?' I ask Ellen with a shake of my head.

'That's pretty tricky,' she admits, and I would laugh if I didn't feel so close to crying.

'The crazy thing is, I still wouldn't know about Fiona if he hadn't been hit by that car. I'd still be going on with my life thinking that I had a loving boyfriend and hoping that he would propose to me one day soon.'

'I don't know what to say. I can't believe Paul was capable of doing something like this.'

'That makes two of us.'

We sip our wine in silence for a moment before Ellen asks me a question.

'What do you think you would have done if you had found out about this when Paul was alive?'

'I'd have kicked him out, obviously.'

'Would you? No chance for an explanation?'

'What would there be to explain? He was seeing somebody else!'

'I know, but you guys had so many years together. Would you really be willing to throw all of that history away if there was a chance you could have rebuilt?'

I'm surprised at my sister's suggestion because I thought she would have been as incredulous about things as I am. But she seems to be making out like Paul and I could have worked through this if only he was still around to explain himself.

'I don't get what you mean,' I tell Ellen as I put my wine glass down on her coffee table while doing my best to keep my voice low because the girls are sleeping upstairs. 'There's no way I could have stayed with him after this. How would I have ever trusted him again?'

I stare at my sister, who nods slowly at my words before she leans forward and puts her own glass down beside mine. Then she looks at me with a vulnerability that I haven't seen in her in a very long time.

'I have something to tell you, and I want you to know that I haven't told anybody else this before. But I'm going to tell you now because I think it might be able to help you process what has happened with Paul and not spend the rest of your life hating him and his memory.'

That sounds very ominous, and I wait for my sister to continue.

'A couple of years ago, I found out that Alex had been unfaithful,' she says, and I'm stunned at the admission.

'What? With who?'

'Some woman in his office. He was working away with her one night. Classic, huh?'

'How did you find out?'

'The hotel where he had stayed had called our house phone the day after, and I picked up. They said that they had found an earring in Alex's bed, and they were calling to try and return it to its owner because it looked expensive. But obviously, there should not have been any earrings anywhere near his bed.'

'What did you do?'

'I confronted him about it when he got home that night. Said the hotel told me there had been somebody else in his room, and I wanted to know who it was. Maybe it was the shock of being accused as soon as he came through the front door, but he admitted everything. He told me how he had been stupid. Got drunk. Made a mistake. But it was just a one-time thing.'

'And you believed him?'

'Yeah, I did.'

'Why?'

'I don't know. Because I wanted to? Because I still loved him? Because he might have been telling me the truth, and that meant something? I don't know, but I believed him, and I also believed him when he assured me that it would never happen again.'

'I can't believe this. What did the girls say?'

'The girls don't know. And they will never know. Nobody will. It's between me and Alex. You're the first person I've told, and you'll be the only one I tell. Promise me you won't say anything to anybody.'

I shake my head, stunned to find out that my sister went through something as shocking as this without confessing it to me sooner.

'Promise me, Sarah. I mean it!'

'Fine, I promise! I won't say anything to anyone!'

'Good because it's in the past. I'm just telling you because a mistake doesn't make somebody a bad person, and it doesn't have to erase all the good things that came before it. Alex is a good husband, and he is a great father. Yes, it hurt me to find out what he did, but that doesn't mean everything else is a lie. And it's the same with you and Paul. Those ten years weren't wasted. Your happy memories are still real.'

I get what she is trying to tell me, but it's a lot to process in one go.

'Do you really trust him now?' I ask Ellen, referring to Alex, who has left the house to go to the gym, or at least that's where he told us he was going.

'Yes, because I have to,' Ellen replies firmly. 'For the sake of this family, and nothing is more important than family.'

I can see that my sister is sincere with that, and I guess she really has found a way to move past Alex's mistake and move on without blowing up her whole life and leaving her kids without a father figure around. But while we are siblings, we still have our differences, and I'm not sure I could have been the same way if I had found out what Paul had been doing while we were still together.

'It's different with Paul,' I say as I pick up my wine glass again. 'He didn't just make one mistake. It went on for years. That's way worse than what Alex did.'

'Maybe, but my point is that you don't have to spend the rest of your life thinking that everything was a lie. Sure, he did things he shouldn't have when he was away from you, but when he was with you, so much of that would have been genuine. You deserved to be loved, and you were loved. I could see how much Paul cared for you.'

I roll my eyes because it seems a pretty hollow thing to say after finding out what I have, but maybe my sister is right. In time, I might be able to see that not everything was a lie with Paul. It will take me a long time to get to that point, and it will be very difficult, but if Ellen can do it with Alex, then maybe I can do it with Paul.

'One day, you will meet somebody else,' Ellen tells me with a sincere nod of the head. 'And they will start with a blank slate. But you need to make sure that you give them that chance, and you won't do unless you have got over this with Paul. You need to learn to trust again, or you'll never be able to have a relationship in the same way.'

This is what I mean about my sister. She might lack common sense, but she does give some pretty heavy advice when it comes to more serious things in life, and I know that what she is telling me is true. I can't hold onto my hate and jealousy over Paul and Fiona forever because it will just cloud my emotions when I do eventually move on.

'Thanks, sis,' I say as I reach across the sofa and give her hand a squeeze, not just for me, but for her because she has obviously been through some tough times in her own relationship too.

'Okay, that's enough about men for one night,' Ellen says as she finishes her drink and reaches out to take my empty glass. 'How about some more wine?'

22

My sister's offer of more wine was gratefully accepted and then some, and that's why it's now approaching midnight as I stumble out of her house and make my way to the car on the driveway. But it's not my car I'm heading towards because I'm clearly in no state to drive. Instead, it is Alex's motor because he has offered to drive me home this evening so that I won't have to pay for a taxi. I say offered, but it was actually more that he was told by Ellen to take me home, but either way, I make it into the passenger seat of my brother-in-law's car before giving my sister a wave and watching Alex come and join me in the vehicle.

Ellen closes the front door to their house as Alex starts the engine, and I lean back with my weary skull on the headrest of my seat as he reverses us off his driveway and gets us moving along the dark, quiet residential street.

It will take less than ten minutes to get to my place from here, and the taxi wouldn't have cost very much at all, but it was nice of Ellen to offer me a free ride home, although I'm not sure her husband was too thrilled about it. It is late, and he has work in the morning, so I'm sure he would rather be tucked up in bed than driving through the chilly streets of our hometown, but he was too polite to say no and call me a taxi instead. He didn't seem thrilled either when he got back from the gym earlier and found Ellen and I had opened a second bottle of wine, but we needed our girly chats, so he had made himself scarce upstairs for the next few hours. But now the night is coming to an end, and what a night it has been. Not only did I get plenty off my chest, but Ellen shared some things with me too, and finding out that her marriage wasn't as perfect as I thought it was certainly came as a shock to me.

Being told what Alex did with that woman from his office is definitely the reason why I feel a little awkward around him now as I sit beside him while he drives me home. I would have thought the wine I had consumed tonight might have made me less edgy around him, but as we go on, I find myself feeling more and more like I need to say something to him about it. Is that wise? Definitely not, but then how many wise decisions were ever made after several glasses of wine?

I'm just about to tell him that I know what he did to my sister when he tells me that he misses Paul and was thinking about him earlier today.

'You were?' I ask him, and he nods his head as he turns the steering wheel, and we round another corner.

'Yeah, I was just thinking about that barbecue we had last year. You remember the one we had during the World Cup? He was on top form that day, wasn't he? So funny.'

Alex chuckles to himself as I think back to the time he is referring to, and I can recall it because it wasn't that long ago, and it was a great day. The weather had been perfect, and we had all enjoyed copious amounts of hot dogs, burgers and chicken wings that had been expertly cooked by Alex and Paul, while Ellen and

I had played with the girls and soaked up the summer sun.

'Remember he told that joke about the one-armed pirate? How did it go again?'

'Why is pirating so addictive?' I say, recalling the cheesy joke that Paul had once told. 'Because once you lose your first hand, you get hooked.'

Alex laughs because it is one of those jokes that is so bad that you have to laugh, and I smile too, still mad at Paul but also able to remember the good times.

'He did love a bad pirate joke, didn't he?' Alex says as we stop at a set of traffic lights.

'Oh yeah, he had plenty of them,' I reply, winding my window down a little so I can get some fresh air into the car.

'The girls loved him. They still say some of his jokes now,' Alex tells me as we drive on. 'They miss him a lot.'

I look at Alex beside me as he drives on, and he nods his head, letting me know just how much his daughters have struggled since Paul disappeared from their lives. He had been a permanent fixture in it ever since they had been born, and he was great with them, always playing and making them laugh and happy to babysit them with me whenever Ellen and Alex needed a night off. It breaks my heart to think of Molly and Bethany wondering why Paul is in the sky with the angels now and if he was in pain before he died. But there's no easy time to grieve somebody, and while it's difficult as a child, it doesn't get much better when you're an adult.

It's obvious as well now that Alex is missing Paul too, and while they were friends, I had always thought it was more just because they were the partners of a pair of sisters. I didn't realise Alex was as fond of Paul as he is making out, but it is nice that he is. I guess they did make plenty of memories together, from all the double dates we went on as a foursome to the few times they went to the pub together while Ellen and I set the world to rights at home. I've been so embroiled in my own grief and search for answers that I haven't really considered how many lives Paul actually touched and how those people are feeling since he left us.

I decide then that I won't mention what Ellen told me tonight to Alex, which is definitely for the best and will mean I have less to regret when I wake up in the morning. There's no doubt that Ellen would have gone mad at me if I had told Alex that I knew what he did because she only told me it to make me feel better about Paul's infidelity, not for me to go and stir up any dramas. There would be little to gain from me acting like the big sister and having a go at Alex for hurting Ellen, so I will leave it, although the truth will always be there embedded in my brain now, and there's no way of knowing for sure if I won't feel like bringing it out again one day. But for now, I will sit quietly and let Alex drive me home in peace, and because the roads are so quiet at this time of night, it doesn't take him long at all to reach the top of my driveway.

'Here we go,' he says, bringing the vehicle to a stop and glancing out of his window at my dark house a few yards away.

I stare at it for a moment too, and there's no doubt that my property isn't very inviting in the way it looks right now. It won't get much better when I go inside because even though I can turn a few lights on, it will still be empty, and I'll still be curling up in my bed alone.

'Do you need a hand getting inside, or are you okay?' Alex asks, probably not because he wants to be a gentleman but because he feels like he has to at least try.

'I'll be fine. I'm not that bad,' I tell him with a laugh before opening my door and taking a very long time to step out onto the concrete.

'I'll see you soon then,' Alex calls to me as I get out of the vehicle, and I thank him for the lift before closing the door and heading for my house.

The car at the top of my driveway waits as I fumble around in my handbag for my front door key until I eventually find it and jam it into the lock. Alex drives away once he has seen me go inside safely, and I think about how that was nice of him as I make my way into my kitchen for a much-needed glass of water.

I turn on the tap and go to get a glass from the cupboard, but before I can complete the task, I freeze because there is something very wrong here.

It's much colder in this room than it should be, and the reason for that is the back door is ajar.

I rush towards it to check that it really is open and not just some figment of my drunken imagination, but it is definitely open, and not only that, but the handle is damaged. It looks like somebody forced it open.

It looks like somebody broke in.

I instantly stop moving and stay as quiet as I can as I listen out for any other sounds in my house, afraid that the intruder might still be here somewhere, ready to jump out and attack me.

A few tense moments pass by without a single sound from anywhere in my home, and I wonder if whoever was here has left already. But I can't be sure, so I grab my mobile phone and dial 999, eager for a police officer or two to come to my house and let me know for certain if I am safe or if somebody is still lurking in an upstairs room.

I tell the female operator who answers my call that I have come home to find evidence of forced entry, and I am worried that somebody might be in my house, and she asks me for my address before telling me that somebody will be with me very shortly. But then she asks me if I have noticed anything missing, and while I haven't yet, that's only because I haven't really checked.

'I'm not sure,' I tell her as I creep through my kitchen and peer around the doorway into my living room, and it's a relief to see that my television is still there, as is my music system on the shelf in the corner. They are the most expensive things I have around the house, barring some jewellery upstairs, but I'm not going to go up there and check the upper level by myself until I have a policeman with me, so I'm just about to tell the operator that I can't check everything when I remember the valuable item I have in my dining room.

Heading for that door, I keep the operator waiting as I peer around it and look at the table in the centre of the dark room.

That's when I realise that something has been taken.

Paul's laptop is gone.

23

The arrival of the police officers at my house has made me feel better in the sense that I'm no longer worrying about being attacked by a mystery intruder. That's because the officers have checked the entire house and have assured me that whoever was here earlier has now left. But I don't feel better in the sense of knowing that whoever did break in here tonight only seemed to be after one thing. They ignored all the other valuables, including my jewellery, which was in plain sight on my bedroom dressing table and instead seemed to have come for only one thing.

The laptop.

The fact that I have no idea why is almost as troubling as not knowing who broke in here this evening.

'So you say that you were at your sister's all night?' Officer Thompson asks me again, going over the notes that he has already made the first time I answered his questions.

'Yeah, I got back at midnight,' I tell him. 'And I noticed the door straight away.'

'And you say that nothing else has been taken other than the laptop?'

'No, as far as I can tell.'

'That's strange.'

I have to agree with the policeman's assessment, but it doesn't help explain it.

'Was there anything particularly valuable on the laptop?' he asks me. 'Confidential work files or information about any assets you might hold?'

'No, nothing like that,' I say, shaking my head.

'And the laptop was your personal one?'

'Yeah,' I say before catching myself and realising that isn't strictly true. 'Well, actually, it was my boyfriend's.'

Officer Thompson looks up from his notepad, his eyes studying me through the lenses of his glasses.

'Your boyfriend's? And where is he?'

'He's, erm…'

I stall on answering that question because I know the answer is going to sound so blunt when I give it. But I'm talking to a policeman, so I can't be dancing around the facts.

'He's dead,' I tell him. 'He got hit by a car a few weeks ago.'

'Oh, I'm sorry,' Officer Thompson says, and he quickly averts his eyes back down to the notepad where things are less awkward. 'What did your boyfriend use the laptop for?'

'Just personal use,' I reply. 'Occasional work emails but mainly just for browsing the internet and storing photos.'

I don't mention the fact that many of those photos were of my boyfriend with another woman, nor the fact that I paid somebody £500 to access those photos for me. I'm sure the policeman would be very interested to know about Calvin and the kind of 'services' he offers, but I won't be grassing that teenager up today because to do so would surely land me in trouble too.

‘So there’s no reason you can think of why somebody would want to take the laptop?’

‘No.’

‘None at all?’

‘No.’

I reply firmly enough to let Officer Thompson know that he can stop asking me that now, and he gets the message before he closes his notepad and stands up to leave.

‘Okay, we will look into this, and hopefully, we will be able to find the laptop for you and return it,’ he says as I stand up with him. ‘We can’t guarantee that, but we will do our best.’

‘I understand.’

‘In the meantime, have a think about if there could have been anything on the laptop that a thief would want to take. I know you have told me that you can’t think of anything but keep trying because if you can, it could be a massive help in our investigation.’

‘Okay, I will,’ I reply as I lead the officer to the door, not expecting to be able to think of anything more that could help him and his colleagues but determined to do my best just in case.

‘And I’d get that back door fixed as soon as possible,’ Officer Thompson tells me as he steps through my front one and joins another officer outside who has been hanging around out there ever since the police car arrived half an hour ago.

'Already on it,' I tell him before they bid me goodbye and head for their vehicle.

I watch them drive away, feeling slightly safer now than I did before until I close my door and think about what I need to do next.

I do need to get the back door fixed, but I also need to let Ellen know what happened tonight while I was at her place. She will most likely offer for me to sleep at hers, and I might just take her up on that offer because I think I will rest easier there than I will here. She did invite me to stay over before Alex drove me home, but I didn't quite like the idea of my nieces running into the spare bedroom at six AM and waking me up, so I politely declined and came home instead. But it's a good job that I did because if I hadn't then I still would have no idea that somebody had broken in here tonight.

I use the internet to help me find an emergency locksmith who might be able to fix my back door, and after calling them, I go to call Ellen before realising how late it is now. It's gone one AM, and she will definitely be asleep, as will Alex and the girls. I have no doubt that she would jump straight out of bed if I was to tell her what happened, but I don't want to cause chaos in her house tonight, so I'll leave it until the morning.

I pour myself a glass of water and go and sit on the sofa while I wait for the out-of-hours locksmith to arrive and charge me a fortune for whatever work he needs to do. While there, I scroll through the television channels, optimistically looking for something half decent to watch at this ungodly hour of the night. But unsurprisingly, there isn't much worth viewing now because most of the population of England is asleep, so I'm just about to give up and turn the TV off when I pause on one of the news channels that runs 24/7.

The poor chap behind the desk giving the bulletins looks like he is disappointed to have worked so hard at journalism school only to end up being assigned the graveyard shift, but he plods on with his task anyway and keeps going through the latest news. That's how I find out that there has been another sorry development in the sad case of the missing young student, Charlotte Graham. Having recently passed the one-year mark since she was last seen, it seems there is further misery for the woman's family to deal with because her brother has just taken his own life. The broadcaster reads out his name, which is Oliver, but I already knew that because I remember seeing Oliver in some of the news footage when Charlotte's disappearance was all over the media. Oliver was twenty-two at the time his sister went missing, but he was twenty-three when he apparently ended his life, battling mental health issues no doubt exacerbated by what might have happened to his sibling.

As screwed up as my own life is right now, and even with the fact that my home has just been broken into, I feel like nothing must be able to compare to the pain that Charlotte and Oliver's parents are going through. They've lost both their children now in tragic circumstances, and that is not something that should ever happen. There's no joy to be found in knowing there are people in the world having a harder time of it than I am though, and if anything, this sad news story tonight only makes me feel even more pessimistic about the world.

It's easy for people who are doing well to say 'cheer up' or 'seize the day', but try telling that to the Graham family now. They would most likely punch that person in the face, and I wouldn't blame them for doing so. It's just like how I have wanted to punch plenty of people in the face since my life unravelled before my eyes too. Maybe I should have punched Fiona in the face. That might have been fun. It certainly would have made me feel better for at least one second about all those stupid photos of her with Paul on his laptop.

His laptop.

Why the hell has somebody broken in here to steal it? What could possibly be on it that would result in somebody needing to get hold of it for themselves? Could it just have been some petty thief breaking in and taking the first thing he saw without bothering to steal anything else? Or could there have been something else on that laptop that I missed?

Something important.

Something confidential.

Something incriminating.

24

I didn't ever expect to find myself back at the computer repair shop in the town centre again, but here I am, ducking out of the rain outside and going into the same store where I first came to try and have Paul's file unlocked. I'm back here because I am wondering if the teenager who helped me the last time I visited can help me again. I'm here to see Calvin, and if he can help me, then I am here to give him some more money too.

I recognise the female employee behind the counter as the same woman who I spoke to on my first visit here, and while she didn't help me that time, I have a much easier question to ask her now.

'Hi. Is Calvin here?'

The woman looks at me like I'm the first ever customer to come inside and request that particular employee specifically.

'Calvin? Why?'

'He helped me with my computer the other day, and I just need to ask him something else about it.'

'I'm sure I can help you with it.'

'Thanks, but it would be easier if I spoke to Calvin. He already knows what the issue was.'

'I remember what your issue was. You needed somebody to help you open a file that had a password on it, right?'

Damn, this woman has a good memory.

'Erm, yeah, that was one thing. But there was something else,' I say, not wanting to dwell on this topic in case she suspects that Calvin might have helped me do something that he shouldn't have. 'If you could just get Calvin, then I could talk to him about it.'

'He's not here. He has Fridays off.'

'Oh, right.'

Damn it. That's annoying. I guess I'll have to come back another time.

'Is he in tomorrow?'

'Yeah, he should be. Unless he phones in sick again.'

The way the woman utters the word 'sick' makes it clear that he obviously isn't sick when he phones in to get out of work and is instead probably just hungover.

'Okay, great. I'll come back tomorrow then,' I say, turning away from the desk. Thank you!'

I scurry out of the shop before the woman can ask me anything else about what business I have with her colleague, and it's not long until I'm back out on the rain-soaked street and heading for where my car is parked.

It's irritating that I didn't get to speak with Calvin today, and even if I had, it might have ended up being a waste of time because he might not be able to help me anymore, but I spent all last night thinking about it, and I have to try. Paul's laptop might be gone now, and the police seem to have no idea where it could be, but Calvin said something to me the other night when he was working on it that makes me hope he might have a way of locating it. He said that he was downloading software onto the device and that it would allow him to do anything on it, including crack the password, and I'm wondering if that same software would now give him the opportunity to track the location of where the laptop could be.

These days, there are all sorts of clever technological applications that allow people to see where devices are. 'Find My Phone'. 'Find My Friends'. They all work by allowing a user to see the exact location of a phone, tablet or computer in case it gets lost or stolen, or simply because they want to find out where their partners or children are. If you know where somebody's phone is then it's a good bet that its owner is in that place too. It's a long shot, but maybe Calvin will have some way of tracking Paul's laptop, and if he does, it would be huge because it wouldn't just mean that I could find out where it was. It would also mean that I could find out who had taken it.

Then I would be able to answer the really important question.

Why?

But that will have to wait until tomorrow when Calvin reports for work again, so I decide that I will try not to dwell on it too much until then. With all the crazy goings-on lately, I feel like my performance has been slipping at work, so I will cut short my lunch hour now and go back to the studio and put in some solid hours doing the job I am paid to do.

I reach my car and get in behind the wheel, glad that I'm able to drive myself around now instead of relying on my brother-in-law like I did last night. I'm still a little groggy after overindulging on wine yesterday with my sister, and I'm more than tired after having such a late night waiting for somebody to come and fix my back door, but it is good to be out and about and staying busy now.

Driving out of the car park and heading in the direction of work, I turn on the radio, looking for some kind of a cheery song to brighten up my journey and my mood. But I end up catching the local news instead, and when I do, I hear the name of the man who was responsible for sending my life into a tailspin.

'Elliot Hargreaves was rushed to hospital after being found unresponsive at his home address this morning, and his condition is currently described as critical but stable. Elliot was currently out on bail awaiting an investigation into his involvement in a fatal traffic accident on Squires Road on the ninth of July, in which local man, Paul Barber, lost his life. It was believed that Elliot was due to plead guilty to the charges of reckless driving against him when he was scheduled to appear in court next month, but that date is now in question.'

I pull over to the side of the road, almost hitting another car in my haste before I bring my vehicle to a stop and grab my mobile phone out of my handbag. I'm calling the officer in charge of Paul's case, and I want to know why I have only just found out about Elliot's situation over the radio. Did the guy try and kill himself so that he doesn't have to face a jail term for driving into Paul? It sounds like it, but I need some concrete answers, and I need them now.

As I wait for the officer to answer her phone, I hit my free hand against the steering wheel, letting out just a tiny bit of the frustration that is boiling up inside of me and threatening to overwhelm me if things don't calm down soon.

The grief of losing Paul. The devastation of finding out about Fiona. The shock of the break-in at home. The mystery of the stolen laptop. And now Elliot, trying to avoid facing Paul's family in court to explain the actions that took another man's life. Things just seem to be getting crazier, not calmer, and I'm not sure how much more of it I can take.

Little did I know it at that time, but all the events of the past were just the tip of the iceberg for what was to come next.

25

I'm sat at my dining room table twirling my fork absent-mindedly through a bowl of tuna pasta on a lonely Friday night, and if things sound bleak, it's because they are. I could have ordered a takeaway and tucked into a much more exciting meal than this one, but I'm trying to cut back on my spending after paying for the expensive locksmith to repair my back door. I'm also aware that Calvin might want more money out of me if he is able to help me track the stolen laptop, and that will be on top of the £500 I have already given him, so best to save money on other things where I can. Of course, I could just not bother trying to get Calvin to help me and forget all about the laptop, but that would mean never knowing why somebody felt it was important enough to steal, so I might as well try and find out, even if it means living off cheap meals for the next few weeks.

But it's not just my unappetising meal that has me feeling downbeat tonight. It's also because I spoke to the officer in charge of Paul's case, and they confirmed to me that Elliot had tried to take his own life ahead of his scheduled appearance in court to face his charges. It was just confirmation of what I had gathered from the news on the radio, but it was another blow because I know how much it would have hurt Paul's parents to know that the man who killed their son had been trying to escape his fate. It could be argued that he wasn't really escaping anything by ending his own life, but I do know that both John and Ruth want to see Elliot face the justice system, and that was almost stopped by what has just happened.

It sounds like Elliot will pull through, which means Paul's family and friends will get to hear the driver's full version of events in court eventually, and I will be there to hear it too. That's because it will look strange if I'm not there as his girlfriend, even though I have since learnt many things about Paul that have tainted everything that we had together. But apart from Ellen, I haven't told anybody about Paul's affair, and I plan on keeping it that way. I might know now that he wasn't a perfect man, but nobody else has to, including his parents, who are still suffering greatly. It won't do any good to let them all know that Paul was capable of lying and keeping sordid secrets, so I'll let them spend the rest of their lives thinking of him without all that negative stuff clouding their memories. That's why I will be in court when the day comes to see Elliot given his sentence, and I'm glad it will still be happening once the driver has made a full recovery, of course.

I'm just about to give up on my meagre meal and carry it into the kitchen, where I will be glad to tip it into the bin, when I hear a knock at my front door.

I put down my knife and fork, not that I was using them much anyway, and wonder who it could be that is visiting me. It's not that late on a Friday night, but it's not so early that a family member or friend might think to casually call around and see if I'm free, so I'm very unsure as I get out of my seat and walk into the hallway. If I had to guess, then I would say that it's Ellen coming to check up on me, but I rather hope not because

I could just do with an early night, and that won't happen if she is here, and especially if she has brought wine. But then I open the door and see that it is not my sister standing on my doorstep.

It's Calvin.

'Oh, hi,' I say, wondering how this teenager could have found me but then quickly remembering that he's already visited my home before.

'Hey, how's it going?' he replies with all the nonchalance of blissful youth. He's even chewing gum when he says it, so casual that it looks like he doesn't have a care in the world, and maybe he doesn't because he is only eighteen after all. Oh, to be his age again.

'Erm, what are you doing here?'

'I heard you were looking for me at the shop earlier today.'

'Yeah, I was. But they said you weren't there, so I was going to come back tomorrow.'

'That's okay, I thought I'd come to you. I got told you had been in the shop, so I figured you must have something else you need hacking on your laptop.'

I presume Calvin has come here eager to make some more quick cash, and maybe he can, but first, I need to explain to him what the situation is, and I wasn't expecting to have to do it here.

'Come in,' I tell him, ushering him through my door and closing it before any of the neighbours can peek out of their curtains and see me with him because they might start wondering what I am up to, and I'm still not 100% sure if what Calvin did for me earlier was illegal or not.

'So, what's happening?' he asks me as he looks around my hallway that is cluttered with discarded shoes and coats.

'The laptop has been stolen.'

'What?'

'The one you worked on for me before. Somebody broke in and took it.'

'What? Who?'

'I don't know. The police are trying to find out, but I'm not expecting much there.'

'Did they take anything else?'

'No, just the laptop.'

'Why?'

'That's what I'm trying to find out, and I'm hoping you can help me. That software you downloaded onto the laptop to help you crack the password. Do you still have all that data somewhere?'

'Erm…'

'Because if you do, you might be able to help me track it, right? If we can see where the laptop is, then I'll be able to find out who took it.'

'Yeah, I get what you mean, but erm…'

Calvin seems very unsure for some reason, but I don't have time for 'erms'. I need absolutes.

'Can you help me find it or not?' I ask him, cutting to the chase.

'Maybe.'

I suddenly realise why he might be hesitant, so I make sure to let him know that he would be paid if he was to assist.

‘How much do you want?’ I ask, the question making my nerves jangle a little because it’s very open-ended, and Calvin could now, theoretically, pluck any number out of the air.

‘I don’t know. I feel bad taking more money off you,’ he tells me, to my surprise.

‘You do? Why?’

Calvin looks around again at the mess in my hallway, and I wonder if he sees me as some kind of crazy woman who lives alone in relative squalor and spends all her time trying to solve computer problems that aren’t really that important. But while the first couple of assessments might be true, the third one is not. This is important. To me, anyway.

‘It really won’t be that difficult,’ Calvin says with a shrug of the shoulders.

‘So you can help me find it?’

‘Yeah, I think so.’

‘Great! What do you need to do?’

‘I’ll have to go and get my stuff. It’s at home.’

‘Okay, can you get it right now?’

Calvin looks a little surprised at how urgent I am asking for this work to be done, but then he nods his head and heads for the door, dodging all my errant pairs of shoes as he goes.

‘I’ll be as quick as I can,’ he tells me, before he pauses on my doorstep and turns back. ‘Have you changed your mind about going for that drink with me?’ he asks rather optimistically before he leaves.

'Don't push your luck,' I tell him before closing the door and leaving him alone with his teenage hormones.

Maybe I shouldn't have been so harsh with him because I do need his help after all. But he is far too young for me. Then again, if he is able to help me locate the laptop so that I can find out who stole it and why then I might have to do something for him. A kiss on the cheek, perhaps. That might be enough to make his day.

We'll see.

But first, I need him to find my laptop.

26

It didn't take Calvin long to go home, get his I.T. equipment and come back to my house, which makes me wonder if he broke the speed limit along the way. He wouldn't be the first teenage driver to take liberties with their car's accelerator pedal. But he's made it back here in one piece, and I'm optimistic about him being able to help me with my problem as he sets up his gear on the dining table and gets to work.

'Are you sure I can't give you any money for this?' I ask him again as he types away on his laptop.

'No, it's fine. You can just get the first round in when we have that date,' he tells me, and I can't help but laugh at his cheeky remark.

'Just concentrate on what you're doing,' I reply with a wry smile.

Calvin focuses on the task at hand for the next few minutes while I quiz him about the kind of software he used to hack the password and will now allow him to potentially see where the laptop has gone.

'The software I installed earlier basically allowed me to go deep into the hard drive on the laptop, and that was how I was able to retrieve the password,' he tells me, speaking slightly slowly because I'm sure he knows that he is talking to somebody with a very limited knowledge of I.T. 'But doing so means I can also see the IP address of the computer and with that, I can see when whoever is using it goes online, and that will tell me where they are.'

That all sounds very helpful for this particular task until I realise that Calvin would also have been able to see when I was using it before it got stolen. He must figure that I've just thought of that particular problem too, because he is quick to dispel my fears.

'Don't worry, I wasn't snooping on you after I left!' he tells me. 'I've done this quite a few times so I've got a lot of IP addresses on here and even though I could monitor them, I'm really not that interested. I've got my own internet browsing to do.'

'That's good to know,' I say, not quite sure if I can believe that Calvin honestly doesn't spy on some of the people who he hacks computers for, but giving him the benefit of the doubt for now. Anyway, if it wasn't for his ability to spy, then he wouldn't be able to do what he is doing for me right here, so I'm grateful for that.

'Okay, I think this is the IP address we're looking for, so I'm going to start the search.'

'Will it be quick?'

'That depends on if the person who stole it is logged in and connected to the internet right now or not. If they are, then we should be able to spot them easily. If not, then we might have to wait until they go online.'

I nod my head, willing to give it as long as it takes to catch this person, and I take a seat beside Calvin as he clicks a button and starts searching.

The I.T. whizz-kid taps his fingers on my table as the search commences while I nervously chew my fingernails and silently pray that this is going to work. And then…

'Got them!' Calvin cries, sitting forward eagerly in his seat and pointing at the screen. 'See that right there? That's your laptop, and it's connected to the internet right now.'

'That means the thief is using it as we speak?'

'Yep, so now all I need to do is find out exactly where they are.'

My heart is racing as I wait for Calvin to give me more information, and as I do, I briefly ponder contacting the police. They would be very interested to know that I have a location on the laptop, and it might be wise for me to get their help just in case it turns out that the thief is dangerous. But then they will want to know how I found out the laptop's whereabouts, and I'm not sure I fancy explaining about Calvin and his potentially illegal ways with them, so I won't call them yet.

I'll sort this out myself, or at least I'll try anyway.

'They're close by,' Calvin says, and he points to the flashing green dot on his laptop, which I assume is representative of my computer.

'How close?' I say, leaning into the screen beside the investigative teenager.

'Very close. Like ten minutes away.'

The map loads up a little more, and now the green dot is flashing on a street, but I can't quite make out the name of it, so I lean in closer. But Calvin's eyes are better than mine, and he tells me the name before I can see it.

‘Wilmore Road,’ he says. ‘I’m not sure on the house number, but I can find it out for you if you just give me a minute.’

Calvin navigates out of the application he is using and goes onto the internet, where he types in the name of the road and brings up a satellite image of the address in question. Then he clicks around on the page, zooming in several times before finally he shows me the photo of the house where he believes the laptop currently is.

‘There you go,’ he says triumphantly. ‘Now, I think you really do owe me a drink.’

Calvin is very pleased with himself, as he should be, but I’m far too worried about what he has just discovered to reply to his sarcastic comment. That’s because I am familiar with the address that he has just pointed to on the screen. I know the road, I know the house, and I know the people who live there. But just to make sure, I ask him for confirmation of the house number on the satellite image on screen.

‘Number four,’ he replies, pointing to the small gold number on the door of the house in the photo.

But I already knew that because I recognised the door in the image anyway. I’ve knocked on it plenty of times before, and I’ve been inside that house plenty of times too.

The location where Paul’s stolen laptop is currently residing is one I know well.

It’s at my sister’s house.

27

I didn't bother telling Calvin that I knew the person who lived at the address he had just given me, nor did I let on how much of a shock it was for me to find out it was they who had taken my laptop. All I had done was usher him out of my front door and close it quickly behind him so that I could have a minute to myself to think.

I had to think about why Paul's laptop was at Ellen's house.

Could she really have stolen it? She did know it existed because I told her how I was trying to access a locked file on it. But why would she want to take it? Unless…

Is there something on there that she doesn't want me to see?

My head is spinning as I stumble to the staircase and scoop up my car keys before turning back for the door. I'm going to go around to my sister's right now and demand to know what the hell is going on here. She might give me some answers, or she might try and deny it, but I won't leave until I learn the truth. I won't leave until I know if she has been doing something with Paul that she shouldn't have.

It sounds crazy to even think it, but why else would she take my laptop unless there was something on the device that could ruin things between her and me? There is the slight chance that she might have taken it to stop me tormenting myself by going through Paul's things and finding more and more damaging evidence that tells me he wasn't the man I thought he was, but would Ellen really resort to burglary just to protect my feelings? I have to think not, so that means I'm thinking there is another more sinister reason for what has happened here.

I leave my house and almost forget to lock the front door in my haste, but I could do without making it easier for any more burglars, so I turn the key in the lock before jumping into my car and starting the engine. I'm on the road within seconds and speeding in the direction of my sister's house, and my right foot's reliance on the accelerator pedal shows how eager I am to get there fast. I'm going way above the speed limit, and I should definitely slow down, but I'm desperate to get to my destination, and that desperation is clouding my judgement. I'm rushing, and because of that, I'm putting myself in danger as well as anybody else who is out here on the roads with me at this time.

I should know better than this, considering I know what it is like to lose somebody at the hands of a careless driver, but I'm not slowing down and I'm barely even acknowledging the colour of the traffic lights that I am hurtling past. I'm just so angry and confused after discovering that the stolen laptop is at my sister's house, and the more I think about it, the more my hands grip the steering wheel, and the more my feet play fast and loose with the pedals.

A light rain has started to fall now as well, adding to the risk that I am taking as I continue to speed towards my sibling's home, and my windscreen wipers start moving in front of my eyes as quickly and erratically as the thoughts are racing through my jumbled mind.

What has Ellen done? Why has she done it? And what does it mean for us in the future?

I hear the sound of a car horn to my left and turn to see a vehicle swerving to stay away from me, but I'm already past it and several metres further down the road before I realise how dangerous that situation was. The fact that I'm getting beeped at by other drivers tells me that I'm not traversing these roads as I should be, and that should be enough of a reminder for me to slow down and make the rest of this journey in a much calmer manner. But then I see the traffic light up ahead, and it's at the stage in its sequence when the amber light has just come on from green. That means that I only have a couple of seconds now until that light turns red, and I will have to come to a stop, waiting impatiently for it to go green again so I can carry on my way. I don't want that to happen, considering how desperate I am to reach Ellen's house, so I put my foot down harder on the accelerator and have a go at passing through the lights before they turn red.

It's not illegal to go through on amber, so I should be okay to make it, but as fast as I'm going, I'm not quite going fast enough, and I see the light turn red before I'm fully through. I'm overcommitted now, so I have no choice but to keep going, but I'm aware that I've just broken one of the cardinal rules of the road, and anything could happen now.

A camera could flash and capture my licence plate details, leading to penalty points on my licence and a possible fine at a later date.

A police officer might be out this evening, maybe in an unmarked vehicle, and they could see what I have done and pull me over before giving me a breathalyser test and admonishing me for reckless driving.

I could end up hitting another vehicle at the intersection, one whose owner has been adhering to the Highway Code and who has gone through their traffic lights on green, only to run into me because I went through on red.

Or maybe, just maybe, I get lucky and I get away with the stupid thing that I have just done in my confused state of mind.

I don’t have to wait long to find out which one it will be and, in the end, it’s none of those options. I don’t get caught by a camera, or stopped by the police, or hit another vehicle, or even get away with it completely.

I end up skidding on the wet surface of the road, and because I’m going too fast, I’m now powerless to do too much about it.

My car aquaplanes across the slick tarmac, and despite my best efforts with both the wheel and the brake pedal, I’m unable to get my vehicle back under control, and the whole world starts spinning outside my window.

After a terrifying few seconds, I veer off the road and only come to a standstill when the car hits a lamppost.

By then, I’m already unconscious.

28

It takes me several seconds to figure out what it is that I am looking at. It's a blue uniform, and it's being worn by a smiling, middle-aged woman with a needle in her hand. I recognise the uniform as one that an NHS nurse would wear, but I have no idea what she is doing being near me with a needle, so I quickly pull away from her and try to get up from where I am currently positioned.

That's when I see that I am lying in a bed, and despite my best efforts, my movements are stiff and laboured, and I think that is down to the fact that my head is absolutely pounding.

'What the hell is going on?'

'Sarah? It's okay, you're in the hospital, but you're going to be fine. Do you remember what happened?'

I stare at the nurse as I think about the answer to her question, but despite my best efforts, I'm not sure that I do remember. I should shake my head to let her know that, but it seems too scary to do so because then I would be admitting that my memory has failed me, so I do nothing instead, as if that is any better. But the nurse rightly takes my lack of a response as evidence that I don't know how I came to be here, so she very kindly helps to jog my memory.

'You were in a car accident. Nobody else was involved, but you skidded off the road and struck a lamppost. Like I said, you're going to be okay, but I'm not sure we could say the same about your car.'

It's all coming back to me now as I process the nurse's words. The speeding. The red light. The spinning around before the sudden stop. And most of all, the reason for all of those things happening in the first place.

Finding out that Paul's laptop is at my sister's house.

'I need to go,' I say, pulling back the bedsheet and making a weary attempt to swing my legs out from off the mattress, but the nurse is quick to stop me from doing that and tucks me back in again.

'Sorry, Sarah, but you're not going anywhere for at least twenty-four hours so we can observe you and make sure that there are no lasting effects from the crash.'

'I'm fine,' I lie, ignoring the dull ache on the right side of my skull, which I will later find out was caused by my head hitting my window when the car came to its abrupt stop.

'No, you are concussed, and you need to take it easy,' the nurse tells me, and her warm smile has made way for a sterner expression that lets me know that she can be forceful as well as friendly.

I realise that I'm better off not going anywhere in my current state, so I begrudgingly stop trying to get out of bed and instead focus on making myself feel a little better in the current moment, which involves me taking a sip of water and swallowing a couple of pills that I have just been handed.

'Your family is in the waiting room. Would you like me to go and tell them that you're awake?' the nurse asks me as I wipe a few water droplets from around my mouth.

'My family?'

'Yes, it's your sister, I believe. We contacted her after your accident.'

That makes sense because I know I have recently changed my emergency contact in my phone to Ellen. It used to be Paul, but there wouldn't be much point in anybody trying to get hold of him these days.

'Ellen is here?'

'Yes, she's in the waiting room.'

'Can I see her?'

'For a few minutes, yes. But only if you feel up to it.'

I nod my head to let the nurse know that I am, but I quickly regret it when my sudden skull movement sends a shockwave of pain coursing through me. But I'm able to cover up the agony well enough for the nurse to not cancel the visit from Ellen, and she leaves the room to go and get my sister while I push myself up in the bed so that I'm now in a sitting position.

I had been on my way to see Ellen before I ended up in here, but now it is her who has come to see me, and it doesn't matter that things didn't go to plan because at least I get to ask her some questions now. She will presumably have some questions of her own, like how I came to be sitting in a hospital bed with my car wrapped around a lamppost in the middle of town. But I won't be giving her any answers until she gives me some of her own.

She is going to tell me why the laptop is at her house, and she is going to do it here.

I impatiently wait for the nurse to return with my sister so I can learn the truth, but it's taking her a while to get back, so I take the time to look around the room I'm in and notice that it is a very bland and very typical hospital room. There's a distinct lack of colour in here because there hasn't been time for anybody to send me flowers, but I'm rather hoping that they won't get the chance to either because I want to be out of here as soon as possible. The nurse said I would be kept in for at least twenty-four hours, but hopefully, that includes the time I have already spent here, although I'm not sure how long that is because I don't remember arriving here, only waking up. I could have been here for several hours already, and I guess it has been a while if Ellen has been able to get here and wait for me to wake up. It's terrifying that there is now a black hole in my memory from after my car skidded and I hit the lamppost, but the good news is that I'm going to be okay, and nobody else was hurt. There will be time for dealing with the police, who will most likely be keen to find out what happened, as there will be for processing the guilt I feel for speeding through the town centre and potentially risking other people's lives. But for now, there is only one thing that is going to happen.

I'm going to make Ellen tell me the truth.

I hear the sound of voices in the corridor outside my room, and while that should be a good thing because it could indicate that the nurse is on her way back with my sister, it's actually bad because the voices don't belong to either of those two people. Instead, they belong to my two nieces, and a second later, I see Molly and Bethany enter the room, closely followed by my sister and the nurse.

'Auntie Sarah!' Bethany cries when she sees me sitting in the bed, and she rushes to my side along with Molly before they both pause when their mother tells them to be careful.

Bethany and her sister look at me like I might be fragile and made out of glass after Ellen's warning, but I let them know that I am okay and usher them towards me for a hug each. Then I look at my sister, who has a very worried expression on her face, and she tells the girls that they can't stay long because I need my rest.

'What happened?' Ellen asks me as the nurse leaves us and the girls to talk for a minute, but I know I can't say much while we're not alone. I also know that I can't ask my sister about the laptop in this situation either because it would be better if that was a private conversation between the two of us. It's very frustrating, but I will get my chance, just not when my little nieces are around.

'I'm fine,' I tell my sister, but the answer is more for the benefit of Molly and Bethany than for her or me. 'How long have you been here for?'

'I don't know. A couple of hours. We came as soon as I got the call.'

A couple of hours doesn't sound too bad when I consider that I could have been unconscious for a lot longer than that, and I nod my head to let my sibling see that I understand. I'm still feeling terrible, both from the accident and from what I discovered just before it, but little children have a way of making anybody put on a front and acting like everything is fine.

'What time is it?' I ask when I figure that it must be past midnight now and certainly far too late for the kids to still be up.

'I don't know,' Ellen replies as she rubs a weary hand over her face. 'But the call woke the girls up, and we came straight here. Alex is in the waiting room too. I tried to get the girls to go back home with him, but they wanted to wait to see you.'

'We were worried,' Molly chimes in, and my heart melts for the sweetness of the little girl who I have kept up late tonight because I was stupid enough to go through a red light.

I can also tell how stressed Ellen has been before she was allowed to come in here because she looks exhausted and not just because of the late hour. God knows what she must have thought when she got the call telling her that her sister had been in a car accident, and I feel terrible for causing her and her family to worry about me. There will be time for me to question her about Paul's laptop, but not tonight. Tonight is about family, and I spend a few more minutes receiving hugs and kisses from my nieces before Ellen tells me that they will leave me alone to get some rest.

As they all leave the room, my sister tells me that she will be back after work tomorrow and will take me home if I am allowed to be discharged. I tell her that sounds good and say I will see her then before waving the girls goodbye and watching them disappear. Then I sink back down into my pillow, resting my throbbing head and thinking about the next time I see my sibling.

The conversation definitely won't be as civil as that.

29

I don't quite feel fully recovered from the head knock I suffered in the accident yesterday, but I've passed the latest round of tests and am allowed to go home, which is all I was bothered about. Now I'm standing at the hospital exit doors waiting for my lift to arrive, and I can't wait to get out of this place. I've always hated hospitals, and that was even before I saw both my parents end up in one and never come out again. I hated them as a child when I would go and sit in A & E with my father after having swallowed something I shouldn't have done or fallen over on the playground and complained of a bruised bone. To me, they're not nice places, and I guess that is just because nobody goes to a place like this unless something is wrong, either with themselves or a loved one, so I'm definitely ready to get out of here now.

But I can't go until my sister arrives.

Where is Ellen? I gave her plenty of notice of when I would be leaving here, and she promised me that she would be on time to collect me, but I still can't see her car arriving in the car park on the other side of these glass doors yet. It's unlike her to be late for anything because she is usually a very timely person, and it's even more strange for her to be late now when she knows that I need her more than I usually would. Does she somehow know that I have some serious questions to ask her when she gets here? Has she found out that I've discovered the whereabouts of the laptop and is now avoiding me? No, I can't see how she could possibly know that I found out about it. As far as Ellen is concerned, this will be a simple pick-up and drop-off.

She has no idea that it will actually be the most testing day of our lifelong relationship so far.

I watch as an elderly man shuffles his way past me with the use of a Zimmer Frame, before making it through the exit doors and out into the fresh air on the other side. Then I see him light up a cigarette and take a deep lungful of smoke, and I guess not even his age, illness and need for better health can get him to quit his most unhelpful of habits. I'm just thinking about how I'm glad that I have never been bitten by the nicotine bug when I see the flash of blue beyond the old man, and I recognise it as Ellen's car driving past.

She is here.

Finally.

I head through the doors and get a strong waft of nicotine as I pass the smoking man before crossing the road to the car park and heading in the direction of my sister's vehicle. She has barely had a chance to get out and buy a ticket from the parking meter when I reach her, and she is extremely sheepish when she sees that the patient she is supposed to be collecting has ended up coming to her.

'I'm so sorry I'm late! There were temporary traffic lights on Ainsley Avenue, so I tried diverting around them, but everyone else had the same idea, and it was just a mess.'

'It's fine,' I say as I put my small bag of belongings into Ellen's boot before making my way around the car to the passenger seat.

'I would have come inside to get you,' Ellen says as she gets the hint that I'm ready to leave and goes back to her own door, but I'm already inside and putting my seatbelt on.

I allow a few moments for Ellen to drive us out of the car park and away from the horrible hospital while I go over what I want to say to her one more time in my head, but just before I can get the words out, my sister speaks first.

'Do you want me to take you straight home, or do you want to go and get some bits from the shops first?' she asks me, turning a corner and taking us onto the main road to town. 'I can pick you up a few essentials now, and then I could go and do a proper food shop later if you would like?'

'Just pull over,' I say, not answering the questions about food because I couldn't care less about eating at this time.

'What?'

'I said pull over.'

'Why? Have you left something at the hospital?'

'No, just pull over, please.'

My insistence eventually does the trick, and Ellen moves the car over to the side of the road before parking and turning to me with a confused look on her face.

'What's wrong?' she asks me, presumably having absolutely no idea at all what is really wrong between us now.

'Why did you take Paul's laptop?' I ask her, getting straight to it.

'What?'

'Don't bother pretending. I know it's at your house. Why do you have it?'

'Sarah, I have no idea what you're talking about.'

'Stop lying to me!'

The volume of my voice is almost as much of a surprise to me as it is to my sister, and I take a second to calm down while I wait for her to respond.

'Sarah, what is going on?' she asks me. 'I thought the doctor said you were okay to leave the hospital.'

'I am!'

'Well, you're obviously not if you're asking me stupid questions like this and shouting at me!'

'Don't blame this on my accident! This has nothing to do with me banging my head! Why do you think I had the accident in the first place? I was on my way to your house at the time!'

'What?'

'I'd just found out where Paul's laptop was, and I was angry. I was speeding, and I went through a red light because I was so desperate to get to your place. That's why I crashed!'

'Oh my God.'

'Tell me why you have Paul's laptop?'

'I don't!'

'Yes, you do!'

It appears that we have reached a bit of a stalemate in the conversation, but I'm not going to back down until Ellen admits taking the laptop.

'Why do you think it's at my house?' my sister asks me after a tense moment.

'I tracked it. You can find almost any electronic device these days if you know how to look. And it told me that it was at your address.'

'That doesn't make any sense.'

'But it's the truth. So why is it there? Why did you take it? Is it because there's something on there that you don't want me to see? Were you having an affair with Paul too?'

'Sarah!'

'Tell me!'

'Of course not!'

'Then why did you steal it?'

'I didn't!'

'Stop lying to me!'

I raise my hand in frustration, and it's as if I want to hit something, but at that moment, I'm not exactly sure what. The dashboard? The wheel? *My sister?*

Ellen recoils from me slightly, clearly afraid that I might be about to strike her, and the sight of her fear is enough to make me realise that I need to calm down quickly or else I should get out of this car before I do something that I might regret. I'm not a violent person and have never hit another living soul, but these aren't normal times. After all the stress I've been under, and after banging my head recently, I feel like a woman at the end of her tether, and Ellen can see that.

'Sarah, please. I don't know what is going on with you right now, but you have to believe me. I didn't take Paul's laptop, and it's not at my house.'

I have to give her credit. She is sticking to her story. But it's still a false one.

'Fine. Keep lying to me. But I know the truth.'

With that, I take off my seatbelt and open the passenger door, stepping out into the road and eager to leave this car and its driver behind.

'What are you doing?' Ellen calls after me as I get out.

'I'm walking home! I can't be with you if you're going to keep lying to me!'

'I'm not lying!'

'Yes, you are. Now open the boot so I can get my bag!'

'No!'

'Do it!'

I remain standing at the side of the parked car, only inches away from where the other vehicles on the road are passing behind me, and this is a very dangerous place to have an argument. I know it, and Ellen knows it too, and that must be why she relents and does what I ask of her, opening the boot so that I can remove my bag from the back of her car.

'Sarah, this is stupid!' she calls to me as I take my bag and slam the boot shut before starting to walk down the road, but I don't bother looking in her direction again.

'Sarah?' she tries again, but I just keep walking.

Eventually, I see her car pass by me on the road, and she has given up for now. That's okay. Now she knows what I know, she will have no choice but to tell me the truth at some point. If not, then I guess that will be the last time we ever speak to each other.

30

It takes me just over an hour to reach my house after abandoning my sister at the roadside near the hospital and trekking all the way across town on foot. My feet are aching, and my head is pounding as I walk down my driveway and take out my house key, but it was worth all the pain to show Ellen how serious I am about finding out the truth. My sister will know now that she has to tell me what is going on, and it's up to her when she does that. The ball is in her court, and if she wants to see me again then she better start telling me what I need to know. I suspect it won't be what I want to hear, but I have to hear it, and time will tell how long it takes for her to be brave enough to do it.

I collapse onto my sofa within seconds of entering my home, and it feels good to take the weight off my tired feet. But I'm going to need something more for my banging headache, and I realise that all the medication I do have to treat such a thing is in the kitchen cupboards, which means I'll have to get back to my feet again if I want any of it.

After forcing myself back up into a standing position, I head into the kitchen and retrieve the medical supplies, popping a couple of pills before ignoring the recommended dosage and popping another two more to go with them. I wash them down with water and wait for them to work their magic, and while I do, I realise that this is probably not the best place for me to be when I'm feeling like this. Paul's things are everywhere. I can't escape him or the memory of what he has done to me, so either I go or his things go.

In the end, there is only going to be one winner.

I rush to the cupboard underneath the sink before pulling out the roll of black bin liners that I keep under there and taking them upstairs into the main bedroom. Opening the first of the fresh bags up, I start pulling Paul's clothes out of the wardrobe indiscriminately, throwing each and every item I can get my hands on into the bag without care for how much it might have cost and how much it might still be worth. It doesn't take me too long to empty all the wardrobes and dressing tables of his things because he was a typical man and only had the bare minimum amount of clothing he needed to get through life, but now that's done, I still have other things that need to be packed away.

The bathroom is my next port of call, and I throw Paul's whole toiletries bag in with the unwanted clothes before scooping up his toothbrush that was still standing upright by the sink as if its owner was going to come back and use it one day. I check the cupboard under the sink because I know that he kept his packet of contact lenses under there, and once I have got them, the only thing I need to do in here then is remove his bodywash and shampoo from the shower. The products he used to keep himself fresh and clean were nowhere as expensive as the ones I use when I shower, so it's easy to disregard them and bundle them in with everything else that will soon be put in the bin.

With the bathroom cleared of 'all things Paul', I go downstairs and start scooping up anything I can find that belongs to him too. His books go in the bin bag, as do his silly little ornaments that he bought on our holidays abroad and the couple of cookbooks he had in the kitchen that he never actually bothered to use.

It doesn't take me long to get everything, and by the time I'm standing by the back door ready to go out to the bins, the bag in my hand is full and heavy. This is it. The contents of a man's life. Ready to be thrown away as if it never even happened.

I can't wait.

But just before I go outside and throw Paul's things away forever, I remember there is one more thing I need to get rid of to make this home a much more palatable place for me to stay. Rushing into the living room, I head for the photo frame on the mantelpiece, the one that holds the image of Paul and I in one of our happy times.

I give it a cursory glance as I pick it up, before dropping it into the bag on top of the clothes, books, toiletries and other miscellaneous things that will soon be out of existence, and then I am done.

Feeling satisfied, or at least as satisfied as a woman can be with a pounding headache and a broken heart, I go out into the back garden and down the side of the house where the bins are kept. There are three of them, all of which are to be used for different recycling purposes. But I'm just going to put this bag in the general waste bin, and I don't care if there's something in this bag that shouldn't go in this bin.

To me, it's rubbish, and rubbish should go to where it belongs.

The dump.

I'm not sure what I was expecting to happen to me after I dropped the bag in the bin, but I didn't get it. No euphoric feeling. No sense of release from my past or freedom for my future. Not even a hint of guilt about being so casual in throwing away my late boyfriend's things. Instead, I just feel nothing.

I go back into my house in a much calmer manner than that in which I left it in, and as I lock the back door, I'm suddenly struck by how lonely I am. Now the house only bears my possessions, no one else's, and having just fallen out with my sister, I realise I'm becoming more isolated by the day. Going to work and seeing colleagues can only do so much for me. I need more company in my personal life, but right now, I feel as lonely as ever.

Perhaps that is why I take out my mobile phone from my pocket. I'm going to message an old friend, any one of them, if only to remind myself that I am not alone and that I can rebuild my life once I have moved past this dark period. But when I do, I see that I have five missed calls on my screen, and they are all from Ellen. Damn it, I put my phone on silent when I turned it on at the hospital, and I've ended up not hearing her calls. But so what? I bet she was only ringing to say the same things she already said to me in her car earlier. I highly doubt she is going to admit to anything over the phone.

But now she is ringing me again, and it's obvious that she is desperate to speak with me, even if it's only to check that I have made it home safely.

I decide to answer her sixth call but am fully prepared to hang up unless she tells me what I need to hear, so I put the phone to my ear and start speaking.

'What?' I say, my greeting dripping in disdain.

'Sarah! Why weren't you answering the phone?'

'What do you want?'

'I need to see you.'

'Not until you tell me what is going on with the laptop.'

'That's what I need to see you about.'

'I don't want to hear any more lies. I know the laptop is at your house.'

My thumb is poised, ready to end the call should my sister try and deny it again. But she doesn't. Instead, she admits it.

'You're right,' she says, her voice quiet and distant at the other end of the line. 'Paul's laptop is at my house.'

31

With my damaged car currently sitting in a scrapyard somewhere, waiting to be crushed into a cube, I had no choice but to take a taxi to my sister's house after I got off the phone with her. I wanted to get to her as quickly as I could before she changed her mind about admitting the truth about the laptop to me. I was surprised she ended up conceding so easily over the phone, considering how much of a fight she had put up in her car when I first broached the subject with her, but Ellen had been very meek and very humble when she had told me that I was right. The laptop is at her house. And then she asked me to visit her so we could discuss it further.

I felt her admission of honesty deserved my compliance with her request, so I called a cab, and now I am almost there. I'm not sure what exactly is waiting for me when I go into her house, but it better be good. If not, I will simply turn around and walk back out of there again, and it will take a hell of a lot to ever get me to go back after that.

The taxi comes to a stop outside Ellen's house, and I pay the driver before making my way to her front door. My sister must have seen me arrive because she opens the door before I reach it, and when I see her face, I see that she looks very different to how she did when I last saw her. Back in her car, she had looked shocked and angry at my accusations. But now she looks different.

Now, she looks just as worried as I am.

'So, why did you take the laptop?' I ask her before she has barely had a chance to close the door behind me.

'I didn't.'

'What? I didn't come here to be lied to! You told me you had it!'

'I do. But I didn't take it!'

'Then who did?'

'I don't know.'

'Ellen! Tell me what's going on, or I swear to God I'm walking out of here, and you'll never see me again!'

'It must have been Alex!'

My sister's answer catches me by surprise, and it takes me a moment to comprehend it.

'Alex?'

'Yeah. It has to be him.'

With that, Ellen walks away into the kitchen, and I follow her in, still trying to get my head around what she has just told me. She believes it is her husband who broke into my home and took Paul's laptop? I guess that is better than it being her who did it, but it's not any less confusing as to why it happened.

I see Paul's laptop is sitting open on the kitchen table as Ellen takes a seat in front of it and gestures for me to sit down in the empty chair beside her. I do as she wishes, and we both stare at the computer in front of us, the same computer that has become the bane of my life ever since I turned it on just after Paul passed away.

'I came home and looked around the house after I picked you up from the hospital,' Ellen says, without taking her eyes off the black screen before her. 'I didn't expect to find it, but I decided to look, based on what you said to me in my car just before you stormed off.

She pauses for a second before finishing her story.

'I found it hidden at the bottom of Alex's wardrobe.'

'What the hell would Alex want with Paul's laptop?' I ask as I realise that she must be right. Her husband did steal it, not her.

'I don't know. That's what we need to find out.'

Ellen looks at me, and I realise she means for me to log onto the laptop and help her start looking around on it for any clues.

I guess that is the only thing we can do right now, so I sit forward and turn the laptop on before entering the password and pressing ENTER. For a second, I worry that Alex might have changed the password to prevent anybody else from accessing this computer again, but I guess he never thought it would be found in his wardrobe because the desktop opens up, which means the same password worked.

We're in.

'I've got about an hour until I need to pick the kids up from school,' Ellen tells me, and I nod before navigating to the toolbar on the desktop and typing in Alex's name.

I begin the search, hoping that it will be an easy one and we will be able to quickly find whatever there is on this laptop that involves my brother-in-law. But life is very rarely easy for me, and I get another reminder of that when the search completes and tells me that there were no results found.

'Damn it,' I say, but I know not to be dismayed that easily when it comes to this laptop now, so I start looking through various files and folders while asking my sister if she can think of any reason at all why her husband would feel the need to steal this laptop for himself.

'I have no idea, but it can't be good, can it?' Ellen replies. 'Not if Paul was cheating. Do you think it could mean that Alex was cheating too?'

'Let's not get carried away,' I tell her, but it's only to stop my sister from freaking out and calling Alex to ask him. 'You haven't told him that you found it yet, have you?'

'No, I just called you as soon as I had it.'

'Good. We can't let him know until we have found what we're looking for. Otherwise, he could just deny whatever it is, and we'll lose the element of surprise.'

'I get that, but how I am supposed to act like everything is okay with him when he comes home from work?'

'You'll just have to manage it. But hopefully, we'll find whatever it is before then, and we'll know the truth without him having to give it to us.'

I keep searching, and there is plenty to look through, but I don't tell Ellen that I have already been through many of these files before when I was looking through Paul's documents. The chances of me being able to find what it is that Alex is worried about are likely slim, but I keep going anyway.

'How did Alex even know I had the laptop?' I ask Ellen as I keep hunting.

'I told him you had found it and that you were trying to crack the password, but I'd warned you against it,' she replies, and that makes sense. A wife sharing things with her husband. That's a healthy thing to do in a relationship. Too bad my relationship with Paul obviously wasn't at that level.

'He must have gone to my house that night I was round here with you,' I say, thinking back to that time. 'He said he was going to the gym, remember?'

Ellen nods her head, and I can see the hurt she is feeling about being lied to written all over her face. It seems we have both been lied to by the men we trust. But there is one difference. While Paul is gone and no longer around to answer for his actions, Alex is still very much alive, and that gives me hope that we will find out what's going on here one way or another. But it would be better if I could just find out for myself via this laptop, or we will have to ask Alex, and he could just make up some story.

'You don't think it's possible that he took it to stop you tormenting yourself with Paul's things?' Ellen asks me but I shoot that theory down straight away.

'Do I think he committed two crimes just to protect his sister-in-law's feelings? No, I do not.'

'I guess.'

I know my sister wants to believe that her partner is innocent, just as much as I wanted to believe that mine was innocent too, but it's become clear now that we have both been involved with men that kept secrets.

'I don't know what there could possibly be on here that could involve Alex,' Ellen says as she watches me keep searching. 'I mean, they were friends but only because they were with us two. I didn't know they were so close as to have secrets together.'

'Neither did I,' I admit. 'But that doesn't mean that there aren't any. We just have to find out what they are.'

And so the search goes on.

32

I've been sitting in front of this laptop for the last three hours, looking for anything I can find on here that might let me know why Alex stole this device from my home. In that time, Ellen has gone out to pick up the girls from school and brought them back home again, and they are now upstairs playing in their bedrooms. I made sure to hide the laptop from them before they came in the kitchen to give me a hug because I don't want them mentioning to their dad that they saw Auntie Sarah around here using a computer that they didn't recognise, as that might tip him off that we are on to him. But it's out again now that my nieces are out of the way, and Ellen is pacing around behind me as I continue to search through it.

'You're sure that he's going to the gym after work?' I ask my sister again, after I glance at the clock in the bottom right-hand corner of the screen to check the time. It has gone six PM, and Alex will be finished at his day job now, which means there is a chance he could come home and catch us here.

'Yeah, he definitely said he was going after work today,' Ellen confirms, and that is good to hear because it should buy us another hour or so to keep looking.

So far, the only things I've found have been the things I've already looked through before. But there must be something on here that I'm missing, and I'm almost certain that there is because I am aware how many places there are to hide things on a piece of technology like this one. I suspect I'm only looking on the surface level right now, and I'll need to go much deeper into the hard drive if I want to find something that relates to Alex. But the problem is, I'm not sure how to.

Ellen has just put the kettle on, and I can hear the sound of it starting to boil as I open more files on the computer and look inside them. But just before the kettle reaches its crescendo and lets Ellen know that the water is ready to be poured into the teacups, we both hear a sound that makes us freeze.

A key turning in a lock.

There's somebody opening the front door.

Alex is home.

'I thought you said he was going to the gym?' I hiss as I leap up from my seat and pick up the laptop, pulling the charger out of it and looking around for somewhere to hide it.

'He said he was!' Ellen whispers back at me as she panics too and almost knocks over one of the cups in her haste to help me conceal the laptop.

I had originally hidden the laptop under the table on one of the chairs when the girls had got back from school, but I feel like we need a better hiding spot for it now, and Ellen obviously agrees because she tells me to give her the computer quickly.

I do as I'm told and watch as my sister scurries away with it into the utility room, where the washing machine and ironing board are kept. I'm not sure where she is planning on hiding it in there, but it better be somewhere good because we are out of time.

'Oh, hi Sarah,' Alex says as he enters the kitchen and sees me standing in the middle of the room.

'Hey!' I reply, slightly high-pitched and a little enthusiastically, but I'm nervous, and my voice tends to go up a few notches when I'm like this.

'How are you feeling?' he asks me, no doubt wondering why I'm up and about at his house so soon after my accident.

'I'm okay, thanks. Feeling much better now.'

'That's good. I thought you would be at home resting for a while yet.'

'Yeah, I was going to, but I've never been a good patient, and I got bored, so I came around here for a cup of tea.'

I gesture towards the steaming kettle and the two cups on the counter as proof of what I have just said, and Alex seems happy enough with that story.

'Great. Where's Ellen?'

'Hi, love!' my sister calls out as she leaves the utility room and closes the door behind her. 'I was just putting a wash on. I thought you were going to the gym?'

'Yeah, that was the plan, but I forgot my bag, didn't I?' Alex replies with a roll of his eyes.

'Oh no. Are you still going to go?'

'Yeah, I really could do with a good workout after the day I've had. Unless you don't want me to?'

'No, you go. It's fine. I've got Ellen for company, and the girls are happy enough upstairs.'

'Great, well, I'll get out of your way then and leave you two to it.'

Alex gives me a smile before turning and walking back out of the kitchen, and Ellen and I share a nervous glance as we wait for him to retrieve his gym bag and leave the house.

It takes a few minutes but eventually, Alex tells us he's going, and we bid him goodbye before we hear the sound of the front door closing that tells us that we are in the clear.

'That was close,' I say as I gesture towards the utility room. 'So where did you hide it? I really hope you didn't put it inside the washing machine.'

'It's under the towels in there,' Ellen replies, and she goes into the utility room to retrieve the hastily hidden computer.

I double-check that Alex has definitely gone by looking out into the hallway as my sister brings the laptop back and returns it to the kitchen table. But before I can begin working on it again, Ellen stops me and shakes her head.

'We could have just asked him then,' she says to me, referring to the opportunity we just had to ask Alex why he had stolen the laptop in the first place.

'Then why didn't you?'

Ellen's lack of a response to my question shows she is worried about what answer her husband might have for her.

I take my seat in front of the computer again while Ellen goes to finish making us the cups of tea, but as I do, I think about how best to proceed from here. We were almost caught just then, and even though we have time to keep looking for any hidden secrets on this laptop, there's no saying that we will be able to find them before Alex gets back from the gym in another hour or so. What's that saying? Insanity is doing the same thing over and over again and expecting a different result? I've been searching long enough on here, and now it's time to try something else.

'This isn't working,' I say, shaking my head and taking my hands off the keyboard.

'What do you mean?'

'I mean, we're not going to find what we're looking for by looking ourselves. We need Alex to lead us to it.'

'How are we going to get him to do that?'

'I've got an idea.'

33

'I'm starting to think you're stalking me,' Calvin says when he sees me waiting for him outside the computer repair shop again.

'You wish,' I reply, before cutting the chit-chat and getting down to business. 'I have something else I need you to do for me. I need you to install some spyware onto a laptop.'

'You're joking?'

'Nope.'

'I'm not sure I can help you,' Calvin tells me rather unexpectedly, and he turns to go back into the shop, suddenly eager to get away from me.

'Wait! Where are you going?'

'I can't help you anymore. Sorry.'

Calvin disappears back inside the shop, leaving me standing alone out on the street feeling very confused.

I have no choice but to enter the shop and pursue him, even though I know he prefers it if I don't talk about his 'extra-curricular' I.T. activities inside his workplace. When I go inside, I see him standing by some of the shelves on the far side, taking printer cartridges out of boxes and putting them out on display. Based on the technological expertise that I know this young man possesses, it does seem like rather a waste of his abilities to have him stacking shelves, but if he would only listen to me, then I could offer him some much rewarding work.

'Hey, what's wrong? I thought you liked helping me?' I say to him when I reach him at the shelves.

'That was when I thought you were being honest with me,' Calvin replies, but that only makes me more perplexed.

'What are you talking about?'

'I'm talking about the fact that you're obviously undercover or something, and you're trying to catch me out by giving me all these different jobs.'

I can't help but laugh at the suggestion.

'Undercover? What do you mean?'

'I don't know. Like you're with the police or something. I thought you were just a nice lady who needed some help, but now you're back here again talking about spyware. That's not a normal thing for someone like you to ask for.'

'I can assure you that I'm not undercover, and I'm not with the police,' I reply, doing my best to keep a straight face as I say it.

'I don't know,' Calvin says with a shake of the head. 'I think you should try asking somebody else.'

'But I trust you. You've helped me before, and I know you can help me again.'

Calvin is still sceptical and looks like he needs a little more convincing.

'Look, if I was undercover and trying to catch you out like you say I am, then wouldn't I have already arrested you by now. You did hack a password for me.'

'Sssshh!' Calvin urges me, and he glances nervously over at the counter where one of his colleagues is standing.

'Look, I have one more thing I need you to do for me, and I can pay you again. However much you want this time. I just need it doing.'

'A grand,' Calvin replies without hesitation, and now it's my turn to be sceptical.

'You want a thousand pounds?'

'Yeah.'

'Wow, that's a lot of money.'

'You said you needed spyware, right?'

'Yeah, but-'

'Well, it's expensive. At least the kind I can get you is. But it will work. But what do you want it for?'

'I need to be able to see what somebody is doing on my laptop when they think that nobody is watching.'

'Wait. I thought your laptop got stolen?'

'It did. But I've got it back. I need you to download the spyware onto it, so I can give it back to the thief and see if I can find out what he stole it for.'

Calvin looks at me like I'm mad, and maybe I am. It is an ambitious plan, but it's the best one I've got. Despite searching for hours on Paul's laptop, I haven't been able to find anything that could tell me why Alex would have stolen it. But there must be something on there that he is worried about, and if I can't find it, perhaps he can lead me to it himself.

'Let me get this straight. Someone stole your laptop, and you've got it back. But now you want to give it back to the person who stole it again?'

'Something like that.'

'Wow, I guess you're right,' Calvin says with a shake of the head.

'About what?'

'About you not being undercover. No policewoman would be stupid enough to do something like that.'

I guess my crazy plan is a good thing in so much as it seems to have convinced Calvin that I'm not trying to trick him into doing something that he shouldn't.

'So, can you help me or not?'

'Yeah, I can help you. I finish work at five, and it's my turn to lock up tonight, so if you bring the laptop here after closing, then I will install the spyware on it for you, and you'll be able to see anything that the thief does on it after that.'

'Perfect. Thank you.'

'Now get out of here before anybody gets suspicious.'

I do as the teenager says and leave the shop, but only for a little while. I will be back soon to give him the laptop so he can download his secretive software onto it, the software that will let me watch what Alex does the next time he logs onto it. All I have to do now is go back to my sister's and take the laptop from where it is hidden in the bottom of the wardrobe. We put it back there yesterday before Alex returned from the gym so that he wouldn't know it had been discovered, and that means he still has no idea that we are on to him. Now, the plan is for Ellen to leave him in the house alone once the spyware is installed on the laptop and hope that he takes the chance to log on and show us exactly why he felt the need to break into my house and commit theft.

Alex has a secret, just like Paul had one. What that secret is remains to be seen. But my late boyfriend was a liar. And it looks like my brother-in-law is a liar too.

34

I've done everything that I needed to do to get my plan in motion. I went back to Ellen's and took the laptop from the wardrobe while Alex was out at work. I returned to the computer shop after it had closed and sat with Calvin while he downloaded the spyware onto it. I then returned to my sister's house and put the laptop back in its hiding place, before going home and sitting down in front of the new laptop that Calvin has kindly let me 'borrow' from the shop. Now I am just waiting for confirmation that Ellen has done everything she needs to do too, and sure enough, the message that comes through on my mobile phone a few minutes later lets me know that she has.

"I've just left the house with the girls. We'll be out for a couple of hours. Alex is home alone."

I text my sibling back and thank her for doing this for me because I know how stressful this time is for her as well as for me. She is just as desperate to know what Alex is up to as I am, if not more, but I have urged her to be patient so that we have the best chance of finding out the full truth, and I'm glad that she has put her trust in me to go along with my plan. She has left Alex home alone tonight, and we're hoping that he takes this opportunity for privacy to take the stolen laptop out of the wardrobe and navigate his way to the file that contains whatever information he is so desperate to keep a secret. Time will tell if he does that or if he just sits on the sofa watching football and eating snacks, but I have a strong feeling that he will do what we need him to do, and when he does, I will be watching.

I put my mobile phone down after sending my message, in which I assured my sister that I would call her as soon as I had any news, and then I click on the application that Calvin has installed on this new laptop for me. This is the app that will let me see whatever Alex does on Paul's laptop from now on, and after a quick training session on it from my teenage I.T. geek, I now know how to use it.

The screen is currently blank and giving me no data, which tells me that Paul's laptop has not been turned on yet, but if it is then I will literally get a mirror image of his screen relayed back to my own so I will see every single mouse click and keystroke that Alex carries out on it.

At the moment, it's like watching the most boring movie in the world, but I'm hoping that soon, it will get very interesting indeed.

I take a sip from my glass of wine that I prepared earlier as I wait for something to happen, and as I do, I think about how I will handle things if it turns out that Alex has been cheating on my sister like Paul was cheating on me. It will be a devastating thing to have to tell her, there is no doubt about that, but I suppose it will be better coming from me than from anybody else, and at least she will know that I am able to relate to the pain she feels, having been through it myself. Of course, I hope it doesn't come to that and that Alex is innocent, but everything at the moment is pointing to that not being the case.

A married father of two with plenty to lose wouldn't steal something unless they have a good reason to do so.

I try to think if there is anything that could be worse than cheating that Alex could be looking to cover up, but I can't comprehend anything else. I have considered that Alex might be trying to cover something up that Paul did, something even worse than Fiona and the affair, but that seems unlikely because, like my sister said, Paul and Alex weren't best friends. They were just a couple of guys who got along because their other halves were related, and apart from all the things we have done together as a foursome, I can only recall there being one or two times when the pair of them went to the pub together without Ellen and I accompanying them. There was the time last year when I took Ellen into the city to watch the latest rom-com at the cinema, and I had suggested that Alex and Paul go for a few drinks together at the same time, which they ended up doing. Other than that, there have been maybe one or two other times when they did things together without Ellen or I present, so it doesn't leave much opportunity for them to have become so close that Alex would now feel compelled to protect Paul's secrets after he had died. That's why I firmly believe that Alex took the laptop because he has a secret of his own to hide, and I will do anything to find out what it is, especially if it is one that could hurt Ellen, Molly and Bethany if it came out some other way.

A red light suddenly goes on in the top, left-hand corner of my dark laptop screen, and I almost drop my glass of wine because I know exactly what that means.

Paul's laptop has just been turned on.

Alex has taken the bait.

I hurry to put the glass in my hand down so I can give the events on screen my full attention, and I watch as I see Alex enter the password that enables him to access Paul's desktop. The very fact that Alex knows what Paul's password is tells me that they must have shared that information, and that is even more reason for me to think that these two men were far closer than either I or Ellen realised.

As I see the cursor move across the screen, I realise that Calvin was right when he told me that I would be able to see every single thing that Alex did on Paul's laptop. It's weird sitting here with my hands on my lap while the cursor moves around by itself in front of me, and I see various files being opened and closed on the screen. As I keep watching, it becomes clear to me that Alex is doing the same thing that I was doing when I used the same laptop.

He's looking for something.

But he doesn't know where to find it.

I stare at the screen intently as various files are opened and disregarded before more pages open up, and more folders are accessed. Alex is a fast worker, going much quicker than I was when I was looking for things, but he still doesn't seem to have found what he is looking for, which means I'm still no nearer to knowing what he is hiding.

I send Ellen a quick message to let her know that her husband is indeed on the laptop while she is out of the house, and she replies quickly, asking me what he is doing. But I hold off on replying to her until I can give her a better answer than ***"Not sure."***

But my sister has never been the most patient of people, and she proves it by calling me a few moments later after I have failed to text her back.

'What's happening?' she asks me as I hold the phone to my ear while I keep my eyes on the screen in front of me. 'What's he doing?'

'He's just looking through some files,' I tell her. 'But he doesn't seem to have found what he wants yet.'

'I hate this.'

'I know, but hopefully, it will be over soon. Just try and have a good time with the girls.'

'How can I do that when I have no idea what my husband is hiding from me!'

That's a good point, and I'm not sure what I can say to that. This is very much like when Ellen tried to tell me to forget about what Paul may or may not have done, but I ignored her advice because it was easy for her to say but not easy for me to carry out. Now the roles have reversed, and she is struggling to listen to what I am trying to tell her to do, and I realise that if I don't find out what Alex is doing by the time Ellen goes back home, she is just going to ask him outright, and all bets are off.

But then I see Alex navigating his way through a part of Paul's laptop that I haven't seen before.

'Hang on,' I tell my sister as I watch to see what Alex will do next.

'What is it?' she asks me, growing more impatient by the second. But I don't answer her as I watch Alex open one file, then another one, then another. It seems like he is still as far away from what he is looking for as before, right up until he opens the fourth file in this mystery folder, and then I realise that the search is finally over. The fact that Alex no longer does anything on his screen only confirms it.

My mouth goes dry, and my hand is shaking as I keep hold of the phone and try to tell my sister what I am looking at on screen.

'Oh my God,' I finally muster, and that's about the only way to sum up this situation right now.

Paul and Alex really did have a secret.

And it is far worse than I thought.

35

I see the headlights from the car as it turns onto my street before coming to a stop outside my house, so I rush away from the window and towards the front door. Stepping outside, I scurry up the driveway to the parked vehicle and see Ellen get out of the driver's seat. She closes the door quickly behind her, and while I can see Molly and Bethany sitting inside the car, I figure they must have been told not to get out by their mother.

Both girls wave at me when they see me, and I wave back, but I'm glad they are staying in the car. That's because my sister and I need to talk urgently and privately, and we have to do it now.

'Thanks for coming round,' I say to Ellen as we step far enough away from the car so that we are out of earshot of the children inside it. I'm also keeping my voice low so that none of my neighbours can hear what I am saying, and I don't even have to ask my sister to do the same because I know that she will when she speaks.

'What the hell are we going to do?' she asks me, her body stiff and tense, and her face a picture of worry.

It's no surprise that she is looking like this after what I told her over the phone, and I don't think what I am going to say next is going to make her feel any better either.

'We have to go to the police.'

'What? No!'

'Keep your voice down.'

'Stop talking about the police then! That's my husband you're talking about!'

'And it's my boyfriend!'

'But Paul is dead.'

'So what? It doesn't matter if he was guilty! And why should Alex be allowed to get away with it just because he has a family?'

'It's my family!'

'I know, and I'm so sorry that this is happening, but you need to make sure that you and the girls are safe from him until we find out what's happened.'

'I'm going to go home and ask him right now.'

'No, don't do that!'

'Why not?'

'Because it's too dangerous. You don't know how he'll react!'

'He might be able to explain!'

'Or he might panic and do something to hurt you!'

We're both shouting now, and while the girls in the car might not be able to hear exactly what we are saying, they will surely be able to hear how loud we are speaking, or rather, arguing. I can see Molly and Bethany's little faces peering out from inside the dark vehicle at the end of my driveway, and I turn my back to them and pull their mother in closer to my side.

'Please, you need to be sensible about this. For their sake, as well as your own.'

'I am being sensible. There's no way Alex has done what you think he has done.'

'Then why did he steal Paul's laptop, and how did he know what to go looking for?'

'I don't know! But he can't have done it. He would never do such a thing!'

'Let's leave it to the police to find out. If he is innocent then he'll be fine, right? I can just report it, I don't have to let Alex know that you were helping me.'

'No, please, just let me speak to him first.'

'It's too risky, sis.'

'Please, I'm begging you.'

I look into my sister's frightened eyes, and it breaks my heart to see her this vulnerable. Her perfect family life is falling apart all around her, and if this all turns out to be true then things will never be the same again; for her, Alex and the kids. But that doesn't mean that I should take pity on her and let her do whatever she asks me to because I have to be the rational one in all of this. Ellen is too emotional to make good decisions, but I am not. I am thinking clearly and logically, and I know what is best for her and my nieces, and they are my main concern right now.

'No, I can't let you take the risk of asking him yourself,' I say, shaking my head. 'Not unless I'm there with you to make sure he doesn't hurt you.'

'What if I ask him in a public place?' Ellen suggests. 'Tomorrow. We'll go for lunch. The kids will be at school, and we'll go somewhere busy enough so that he can't do anything to me if it does turn out that he is guilty.'

I think about that plan, and while it's still not ideal, it does sound better than Ellen bringing this up with Alex tonight in the privacy of their own home.

'I guess that could work. But that means not saying anything tonight when you go back home to him. Can you do that?'

Ellen looks unsure for a minute until she realises that she is going to have no choice.

'Yeah, I can do that.'

'Are you sure? Because if not then I'm not letting you go back there, and I'll call the police right now from here.'

'I'm sure! I promise.'

Ellen nods her head to convince me to trust her, and of course I do because she is the only person who I really trust in the world these days.

'Okay, speak to Alex tomorrow, somewhere public, and see what he says. Maybe you're right, and there is an explanation for this, but if not then you have to go to the police. Even if he runs. Even if he threatens you. Whatever happens. You have to do it, and it's not just for your family, do you understand?'

Ellen nods again. She knows exactly what I mean.

'Okay, I'm going to go back,' she says to me, but before she goes, she gives me a hug.

She squeezes me tightly as if she needs every ounce of strength to be transferred from my body into hers before she returns to Alex, and I'm happy to hold the embrace for as long as she needs it.

Eventually, we separate, and I tell her that I love her as she heads back to her car and opens the driver side door. I wave to the two girls in the back seat again as their mum gets in behind the wheel, before Ellen starts the engine and finally drives away.

I take a deep breath once I am back inside my house and try to calm my racing thoughts, all of which are now conspiring to make me very paranoid about what might happen next. Did I make a mistake then by letting Ellen and the girls go back home? Should I have insisted that she stay here until I called the police? Perhaps it's not too late to call them now, and they might even get to the house before Ellen does. But I told her that I trusted her, and I know she trusts me too. That means that I'm not to do anything until she has had a chance to speak to Alex about this new development first, and she has told me she will do that tomorrow lunchtime, somewhere public in case it all goes wrong. I'll have to wait until then to find out what happens next, which means it's going to be a very long night for me. But it won't be anywhere near as long as it is going to be for my sister, who will have to sleep beside a man who might be dangerous.

I thought what Paul did to me with Fiona was as bad as it could get, but I was wrong.

What I saw Alex looking at on my late boyfriend's laptop was worse.

Much worse.

This isn't infidelity we're talking about now.

It's possible murder.

36

I'm surrounded by darkness, and for a moment, I assume I must have my eyes closed. But they're not closed. They are wide open.

I just can't see anything.

A wave of panic washes over me as I worry about my sight.

Why can't I see anything?

Am I blind?

'Help!' I call out, putting my hands out in front of me to feel something that might tell me where I am and, more importantly, that I'm not alone. But I can't feel anything, and I still don't know where I am or if anybody else is with me.

Then I hear the scrape of a foot on the ground behind me, and I spin around to face in that direction, and to my eternal relief, I can now see something. It's not much, just a sliver of pale moonlight shining down on what looks like several brown leaves, but it's better than being in the darkness of a few seconds ago. But I still can't see anybody else here, even though I definitely just heard somebody moving, so I call out to them again.

'Hello?'

There is still no response, only glimpses of silver light shining down from above and illuminating patches of what I am starting to realise is a forest floor.

Being in a strange place like this at night by myself is scary but not half as scary as knowing that I'm not really here by myself. There is definitely somebody here with me, and while I still can't see them or even hear them anymore, I can certainly sense them. There is another presence, and I need them to show themselves to me soon, before my racing heart can't take it anymore and stops beating, leaving me lying in a crumpled heap on this leaf-covered ground.

'What are you doing, Sarah?'

It's a male voice that speaks to me from behind, and I spin around quickly to find out who said it. And then I see him, or rather, I see his smile.

The white teeth stand out when contrasted with the dark background, and two steely eyes stare back at me from only a few feet away. I recognise the eyes, just like I recognise the smile. This is somebody I know well. This is a member of my family.

It's my brother-in-law.

It's Alex.

'What's happening?' I ask him as I see him standing in front of me, his silhouette almost seeming to shimmer in the moonlight that seems to be becoming brighter by the second.

'I'm here to punish you,' Alex tells me, that smile becoming even bigger and even more wicked.

'Punish me for what?'

'For not leaving the past where it belongs.'

I feel as though I know exactly what Alex means by that, and because I do, I take a couple of steps away from him, increasing the distance between us as if that can somehow make me safer in this situation. But I already know it's pointless, and Alex seems to know it too.

His laughter only proves it.

'What are you going to do to me?' I ask him as I keep moving away, walking backwards, not looking where I am going, which is never a good idea and especially not in a dark and dangerous environment like this one…

'Careful there,' Alex says to me, as if warning me about something, but I don't heed that warning, and that's when I suddenly feel the ground give way beneath me.

A gasp of air escapes my lungs as I feel myself falling backwards, completely at the mercy of gravity now and with no idea where I will land.

Thankfully, my fall isn't too big, and only a couple of seconds pass before I feel my back slamming into a soft, slick surface.

Groaning as I recover from the fall, I look around me and see that I am lying on a bed of dirt, and it's one that is flanked on all sides by a wall of dirt that towers above me.

I'm in a hole.

Or a grave.

'Help me!' I cry out to Alex as I hold a hand in the air in the hope that he will take it and pull me out of here.

But he doesn't do that.

He just starts shovelling.

I feel something hit me in the face, and as I wipe my eyes and mouth, I see that it is soil. I'm being buried, and Alex is whistling a tune as he works.

‘Wait! Stop!’ I plead, as if that is going to be enough for the man standing over this hole to have some mercy on me and cease what he is doing. But it doesn’t work. He just keeps using his spade to send more and more soil falling down on top of me, and now I know that there is no escape.

Alex was right. I should have left the past where it belongs. I shouldn’t have gone digging up things that didn’t concern me. But because I did, Alex has now dug this hole for me.

I let out several more cries for help, but the soil keeps on coming, and it isn’t long until I can feel the weight of it on my chest. I continue to wriggle my arms and legs, but I can’t move my torso now, and that means I’m not able to pull myself out of this hole before it’s too late.

This is really happening.

I’m about to be buried alive.

As scary as this is, it still doesn’t feel real while my face is still free. My body is covered by dirt now, but my head is still above the soil, and as long as that is the case, then I will be able to breathe. That means I still have a chance at getting out of this. But then Alex appears at the edge of the hole, and I see that his spade is full of soil and ready to be delivered.

This is it.

The last time I ever get to see the world.

And the last breath I will ever take.

‘Please…’ I try, but it’s as if all the energy has been sapped out of me and I don’t have the strength to fight my fate any longer.

Alex's smile is the last thing I see before everything goes black, and then that is it.

It's over.

I'm going to die.

I suddenly push myself forward as hard as I can, scratching at my face and drawing in as much air as possible to my lungs, fighting the darkness and the soil and the man with the spade. That's when I see that he is gone, as is the hole and the dirty forest floor. I'm in my bedroom now, in my house, and the only moonlight I can see is the light seeping through my curtain in front of the window.

I still have to check the bed I am sitting up in for any sign of dirt and leaves, but as each second ticks by, I realise what just happened.

I was having a bad dream. I'm not really being buried. There is no brother-in-law with a spade, smiling at me as he punishes me for digging up the past.

I'm safe.

The sense of relief I feel is overwhelming as I slowly rest my head back down onto my pillow and wait for my heart rate and breathing to become more relaxed. That was horrible, but it was just a nightmare. But that doesn't mean that it was insignificant. The content of it felt all too real, and that's because I know what Alex might have done. Just because he didn't really bury me just then, it doesn't mean he hasn't buried somebody else before.

I know that I have zero chance of getting back to sleep now, so I reach over to my bedside table and pick up my mobile phone, mainly to check the time but also to find something to occupy my frazzled mind. But as I do, I see that I have received a text message from Ellen.

"We need to talk. Meet me at the park in Bridge Woods at 8am. Love you sis xx"

I text my sister back quickly to let her know that I will be there, even though it's now the middle of the night, and she sent the message a few hours ago while I was sleeping. But she will see it as soon as she wakes up, and she will know that I am going to be at the park in the woods to meet her.

I know the park well because it's the same one where we have taken Molly and Bethany to play over the years, but there won't be any fun on the swings or slides this time. I expect Ellen is going to tell me something about Alex, something she may have found out since I last saw her. While that wasn't the plan because she was supposed to be speaking with him in a public place at lunchtime, I have to go and find out what has happened.

I guess it can't be anything too bad because Ellen's message is serious but not scary. She doesn't sound afraid, just focused.

I guess I'll find out what she has to tell me soon enough.

37

A cold wind is blowing across the park as I stand in the middle of it, waiting for Ellen to arrive. The wind is strong enough to make one of the swing seats start moving, and the two chains it is attached to move awkwardly as if they haven't quite woken up yet.

They're not the only ones.

It's early in the morning, and to make things worse, I failed to get back to sleep after my nightmare in the early hours. That means I'm exhausted as I stand here and look out for my sister, and I hope she isn't going to make me wait too long.

Other than me, there is just a solitary dog walker in this park, and they give me a quick nod of the head as they pass by, that very respectful and very British way of saying 'hi' to any stranger you pass on a walk without actually saying any words at all.

I watch the dog owner walking away from me while his black Labrador ambles happily alongside him, and I wonder what it must be like to be strolling through the park without a care in the world. I can barely remember a time when I wasn't tired, anxious and confused after recent events, and it seems stupid to think that I will be carefree anytime soon.

Not with what I have on my mind these days.

'Hi, Sarah.'

The voice behind me almost makes me jump out of my skin, one, because I didn't know anybody was so close to me and two, because it's not the sound of my sister's voice. It sounded like Alex, and when I turn around, I see that it is.

This is just like my nightmare.

'Alex? What are you doing here?' I say, which is hardly the politest way for me to greet my brother-in-law, but I didn't really have a chance to compose myself and think of something better.

'I've come to meet you,' he tells me, and it takes me a second to get what he means.

'You sent me the text message?'

'That's right.'

I can't believe this. *He pretended to be my sister?*

'Where's Ellen? What have you done to her?'

'Relax, Ellen is fine. She's getting the girls ready for school. But she does want to go for lunch with me later, and it got me wondering as to why that might be.'

I do my best to display a good poker face so as not to give away what I know, while Alex goes on.

'You see, I've been married to my wife long enough now to know when something is troubling her, so I made sure to ask her if everything was alright last night as we were getting into bed. She assured me that it was, but she was obviously lying because, as I'm sure you know too, Ellen is a terrible liar.'

I still say nothing as Alex studies my expression for any hints or clues as to what I might be thinking.

'And then Ellen said something that got me thinking. She mentioned the case of Charlotte Graham and said that somebody at her work had been talking about it recently. She said that her colleague had a new theory on what might have happened to the missing student, and then she asked for my opinion on it. Do you know what I said to that?'

I shake my head in response while simultaneously wondering why the hell my sister would be so stupid as to start probing Alex about Charlotte when she said she was going to wait to be in a public place before doing that.

'I said that I had no idea what might have happened to her, just like the girl's family and the police and everybody else in this town have no idea either. But you know what I thought as we went to sleep beside each other last night?'

I shake my head again as the wind picks up and swirls around the two of us.

'I thought that my wife thinks she knows what has happened to Charlotte now. And that must mean that you know too.'

I look past Alex to where I had last seen the dog walker pottering away, but he is long gone, as is his dog. My brother-in-law and I are now the only two people in this chilly park, and that is not a good thing. This might be a public place, but it's not much good if there are no other members of the public around to help me if I need it.

'I don't know what you're talking about,' I say, hoping that playing dumb will be enough to get me out of this potentially dangerous situation.

'I think that's not true,' Alex tells me with a shake of his own head this time. 'I think you found something on Paul's laptop, and I think you also found out that it was me who stole it from your house. Because of that, I think you and my wife both now know that Paul and I had something to do with Charlotte's disappearance last year.'

Alex has just laid out everything that has happened, and it's the surprise of hearing him relaying it to me that must be the reason why I make a terrible attempt at feigning shock. But he doesn't buy it for a second and steps closer towards me, grabbing me by the arm and telling me what is going to happen next.

'I like you, Sarah, and you know that I love your sister too,' he begins, his eyes boring into mine as his face is only inches away from me. 'That's why I don't want to hurt either of you, and I won't have to if you stay calm and listen to everything that I am about to tell you. Do you understand?'

I nod my head, and it's about all I can do as I'm frozen with fear while in the grip of this man.

'Good. Now, let's take a walk.'

Alex lets go of my arm and starts walking towards the trees at the back of the park, and while I think about turning and rushing away in the other direction, I know that I should follow him. For my sake and for my sister's.

I walk behind Alex as we make our way past the swings and the slide and over the grass that is still slick with early morning dew, before we reach the treeline that leads into the main body of Bridge Woods. The reason for the name of these particular woods is because there is a bridge over a small stream right in the centre of all these trees, and it does make a great spot for a photograph. But somehow, I don't think Alex has brought me here today to help him take a scenic picture.

He stops in front of the trees, so I stop a couple of yards behind him, and I watch as he looks up at the thick trunks in front of him and the long, slender branches that stick out in all directions and make this both a fun and a dangerous place for children to play.

'What are we doing here?' I ask Alex when he fails to enlighten me about his thoughts, and he turns back to look at me before answering.

'This is where we buried her.'

I realise right away what he is talking about, and my hand goes over my mouth to cover my shock at his admission. Alex nods his head before turning back to the trees, and he puts his hands in his pockets before letting out a deep sigh.

'It was the night when you and Ellen went to the cinema to watch that new rom-com last year. Do you remember?'

I do remember, but I say or do nothing, instead just staring at the back of the man who is admitting something terrible to me.

'Both of you were so keen for me and Paul to do something together too, so we got a babysitter, and we went to the pub while you went to watch the film. But I really wish we hadn't bothered.'

'What did you do?' I ask, suddenly finding my voice again, but Alex doesn't turn around to answer me.

'We did exactly what a couple of guys would do when at the pub. We drank beer and then we drank some more. But I drank more than Paul because he had stupidly driven to the pub, so he needed to drive home again. He said he had some important meeting at work the next day so he couldn't have too much, and he had brought the car to make sure that he didn't overdo it. But he had already had too much to drive. I knew it, and so did he.'

'He drove home after drinking?'

Alex nods his head. 'I thought he had brought the car because he didn't want to be out with me, so it was an excuse to make it an early night. I wasn't offended though, because we were never best friends, were we? We just hung out occasionally while you and Ellen spent time together.'

'What happened?'

'Paul offered me a lift home when we left the pub, and even though I knew he was most likely over the limit, I stupidly agreed with him. We got in the car and set off in the direction of my house.'

Alex bows his head, and I can see him shaking it as he recounts the sorry story.

'We were about ten minutes from my place when we hit Charlotte,' he says, while keeping his eyes down at the ground. 'She came out of nowhere. Just crossed the street right in front of the car. Paul slammed on the brakes, but it was too late. We knew from the noise it made that it wasn't good.'

'Oh my God,' I say, feeling a shiver run down my spine as I try and imagine what it must have been like.

'Yeah, that was our reaction too. We couldn't believe what had happened and when we got out, we couldn't believe that the girl was dead.'

'What did you do with her?' I ask, even though I already feel like I know the answer now.

'Paul was panicking because he knew he was over the limit, and he knew he would go to prison. It was his idea to hide the body, not mine. I should have just called the police. But I knew it would mess up all of our lives. Paul would go away for years, you would be devastated, and that would mean Ellen would be devastated too. I wanted to avoid all of that, and so did Paul. So I decided to help him move the body.'

'You brought her here?'

Alex nods. 'I'm not going to show you the exact spot, but I can remember where it is. And you already know what it looks like because you have seen the photo of it on Paul's laptop, haven't you?'

Alex looks at me as I nod my head before asking the question that has been bugging me ever since I saw Alex looking at that photo of a section of these woods, in amongst various articles about Charlotte's disappearance that my late boyfriend had obviously accumulated as some weird way of dealing with his guilt.

'Why did Paul take a photo of the grave, and why did he keep it on his laptop?' I ask, unclear as to why he would do something that would tie him to the crime.

'He said it was in case the guilt got too much for him, and he wanted to go to the police in the future. The photo would help him remember exactly where Charlotte was buried if they needed to go looking. I obviously told him it was a bad idea, and I begged him to get rid of the photo as well as stop reading and saving so many damn articles about her disappearance, but he never listened to me. He felt guilty about it.'

'But not guilty enough to go to the police.'

'I know what we did was wrong, but we panicked, and it was just one mistake.'

'One mistake? You took an innocent woman's life and then covered it up!'

'It was wrong, but think of the alternative! Paul would have gone to prison. Would you have stayed with him after that?'

'I don't know. Maybe.'

'I doubt it, and Paul doubted it too. That was why he kept it a secret. He didn't want to lose you.'

'He was cheating on me!'

I wonder if that will come as a shock to Alex but it doesn't, and now I see that these two men shared a lot more together than just a dead body.

'You knew about his affair?' I ask him as I step closer to him, feeling an anger bubbling up to overtake my shock and sorrow at what I have just been told.

'Yes. I mean, not when it started. But he told me about it after what happened with Charlotte. I guess he felt like I was the only one he could share things with anymore, and he told me about Fiona. But I just told him to end it and to move on with his life like I was trying to move on with mine. If I'm honest, I just wanted him to leave you so I would never have to see him again. But you two seemed like you would be together forever. Until…'

Alex stops talking before mentioning the accident that claimed Paul's life, but it's hard not to think of that accident as some kind of karma for what my boyfriend did to Charlotte.

'When I heard Ellen talking about you snooping around on Paul's laptop, I knew I had to get it before you found the stuff about Charlotte on there. I broke into your house that night when you were with Ellen, but I didn't get around to deleting everything at the time. I had to do it later, and I guess that's how you caught me, right?'

'Spyware,' I say, and Alex shakes his head.

'Damn it.'

'Ellen was going to tell you that she knew today and see what you said.'

'I thought so. That's why I had to meet you first.'

'Why tell me and not your wife?'

'Because my wife still loves me and thinks I'm a good man.'

The wind causes the leaves on the trees in front of us to flutter, and it almost feels as if the woods are trying to shed themselves of their connection to a horrible history. These woods hold a body, the body of a woman who was just trying to get home when she got hit by a drunk driver.

My late boyfriend.

Poor Charlotte. The missing student is buried in the middle of all these trees somewhere, and her family still don't know what happened to her.

But it's time that changed.

'You have to tell the police everything,' I say as I stand beside Alex and look at the cowering man beside me. 'Or I will.'

'No, you can't! Please!' Alex begs, grabbing my hands and clinging to them like a desperate child would cling to their parents on their first day of school. 'Think about Ellen! Think about Molly and Bethany!'

'Think about Charlotte's parents. They have spent the last year in agony, not knowing what happened to their child!'

'I know that, and it's terrible, but it won't bring her back. She's gone, and their family is ruined. But don't ruin my family. *Your family*. Please, I'm begging you!'

I listen to all of Alex's pathetic pleas and think about how much chaos it would cause in the lives of my sister and my nieces if all of this came out. But it has to come out. Doesn't it?

'Please, Sarah. You have to keep this a secret. I love your sister, and I love my daughters. Don't make me lose them. Please.'

38

I might be mad for what I have done, but I told Alex that I would keep his secret safe for the sake of his family. That was enough for him to believe me and walk away in the park, going back to his life and leaving me to get on with mine. I told him what he wanted, or rather needed, to hear, and now he thinks everything is okay again.

But it's not.

How can it be?

I know what he did, and together with Paul, they ruined an innocent young woman's life as well as her poor family's. Charlotte Graham is still classed as missing, and her parents' agonising wait for answers goes on. Unless I put a stop to it and tell them the truth.

Unless I reveal to the world Alex and Paul's dirty secret.

I'm still mulling over what to do as I sit in my home and browse the internet, reading news article after news article about Charlotte and everything that has happened since she 'vanished.' All the theories about abductions, or jealous exes, or her just running away and not wanting to be found. I've been intrigued by all of the ideas about what may have happened to Charlotte over the past year, just like so many other people in this country who have found themselves gripped by the sad but intriguing story. But now that I know the truth, there is no morbid curiosity or burning desire for answers. I wish I'd never heard of this poor woman, or rather, I wish Paul and Alex had never run her over after they had been out drinking in the pub.

It's unbelievable that the man I loved and trusted could not only turn out to be a cheat but a killer too. But if I thought the whole Fiona thing was bad, then this Charlotte situation takes the prize. I get that anybody can make a mistake, even if there is absolutely no excuse for drink driving in any situation, but to hide a dead body and then go on living as if nothing had happened?

How can any human being do that, least of all the man I loved?

But at least my man is no longer around, so I don't have to look him in the eyes and know that he is harbouring a horrible secret. Unlike my sister, who is still very much in a relationship with a dangerous man, who will most likely do anything to stay out of prison.

After assuring Alex that I wouldn't tell anybody what he had admitted to me, he had told me that he would come up with a story for Ellen at lunchtime about why there happened to be so many things relating to Charlotte's disappearance on Paul's laptop and also why he had felt compelled to steal that laptop. Alex said some fiction about Paul having a few dark fantasies and how he felt like he owed it to his late friend to cover them up, but whatever story he conjures up, it's all a load of rubbish. Paul felt guilty about what he had done, which was why he took a photo of Charlotte's burial site as well as read and stored so many articles about the woman he knew he had killed. His guilt doesn't make up for what he did, but at least he showed remorse. Alex just seems to have shown nothing but a cold and calculated way of moving on and keeping himself safe, and it's that streak that worries me the most.

If he is willing to break into my house and steal a laptop to protect his past, what would he be willing to do to Ellen or me if he ever thought we were going to report him?

I check the time in the corner of my laptop screen, the laptop that I borrowed from Calvin because Alex still has Paul's, and I see that it is midday, which is about the time that Ellen told me that she was meeting with Alex in a public place. I believe they are meeting at the food court in the indoor shopping centre in the middle of town, which is about as public a place as one could get, so I feel confident that Ellen will be fine there with her husband, whatever is said between them. But it's my knowledge of where they are right now that means I could go to the police and tell them exactly what Alex has done and where he can be found, and that is a very tempting thought. The only thing that is stopping me from going to the station and doing that is what it would do to my sister to see her husband arrested right in front of her. It would be terrible and not something she would easily get over, and that would be before she even knew what Alex had done.

As our meeting in the park came to an end earlier, I implored him to tell his wife what he had told me and let her decide if she wanted to stay with him or not. But he didn't see that as something he was willing to try, and I can see why from his point of view.

Who would want to stay married to a man who buries women in the woods?

That's why I know that Alex will never tell Ellen what he told me. He obviously needed to get some guilt off his chest with me, and he has done that now, but that's as far as he is willing to go. But by telling me, he has also incriminated me because he knows that I am now withholding information that would be vital to an ongoing police investigation. Perhaps that was his real reason for confessing all along. He knew I was onto him, and he decided to implicate me too, well aware that the longer I didn't go to the police, the worse it would get for me until eventually I would be just as screwed as him and need the secret to lie buried forever.

But I'm not going to let him do that to me.

I've just decided that I'm going to tell the police what he did and I'm going to tell them where they can find him right now.

I put the laptop down on the coffee table and stand up, feeling a little faint as I move but only because of what I am about to do. I am about to walk into a police station and tell the officer behind the desk that I know what happened to Charlotte Graham. I don't expect that I will have to wait long to get seen to after that, and I don't expect it will take long for several police cars to drive over to the shopping centre in town and make an arrest in the food court.

Pulling on my coat and grabbing my car keys, I head for the front door, going over exactly what I need to say and the order I need to say it in in my head. Then I open the door and prepare to step outside, but as I do, I see somebody waiting for me on the doorstep.

It's somebody I really did not expect to see or want to see at this time.

It's Alex.

'What are you doing here?' I ask, freezing in my doorway as soon as I see him standing before me.

'I've come to see what you're up to,' he replies. 'Can I come in?'

'I thought you were meeting Ellen for lunch?'

'Change of plans.'

'What's happened?'

'Nothing. Can I come in?'

'No,' I say, worried about why he keeps asking me that. But Alex doesn't take no for an answer, and before I can close my front door on him, he forces his way inside and shuts it for me.

'What are you doing? Get out!'

But Alex doesn't say anything now.

He just puts his hand over my mouth and forces me into the living room.

39

ELLEN

I check the time again, but I already know it's way past the time when my husband was supposed to be here to meet me. Sure enough, the clock doesn't lie, and I see that Alex is now thirty minutes late for our rendezvous in the food court. I have tried calling his mobile, but there has been no answer, nor has there been any response to my text message that I sent ten minutes ago either. I'm not sure where he is or why he is so delayed, but the longer I sit here, the more I think that he isn't going to come at all. That would be a shame because this was going to be the time when I asked him outright if he knew why Paul had so many things relating to Charlotte Graham on his laptop, including a photo taken in the woods and what looked like disturbed ground as if a hole had just been dug.

It was Sarah's idea for me to have that conversation with Alex in a public place in case he reacted badly when I confronted him, and that's why I am now sitting at one of the many tables in this food court, the rest of which are all filled with families and couples tucking into some fast food before carrying on with their day's shopping. Unlike these other people, I haven't ordered any food yet, though. I have been waiting for Alex to join me, not that I have had much of an appetite recently. It's hard to eat when all you can think about is why your husband has been lying to you and what other things he might have done wrong to go with breaking and entering and theft of a laptop.

I was hoping, and still am hoping, that Alex was going to come here today and give me a perfectly good explanation as to why he stole Paul's laptop and why he knew to go looking for the folder containing the information about Charlotte. Did Paul have something to do with the young student's disappearance? If so, what has Alex got to do with that? Sarah thinks the worst, which is that they may both be the reason why she vanished, but I'm still holding out hope for an explanation that doesn't consist of my husband being a dangerous man.

Paul was a liar, that much is clear now.

But I like to think that Alex is better than that.

I let out a deep sigh and check the time again, but another ten minutes have passed without Alex showing up, and now I'm just about ready to leave here and go home. It's not just the noise from the kids at the nearby tables that is giving me a headache, but the stress of what is going on in my personal life, and I could do with a quiet room to lie down in rather than this frenzied environment.

Getting up from my table, I put my handbag over my shoulder and turn for the door, and a young mother with two very young children are already rushing to take the space I have just vacated. I grimace at the mother as I pass her by, jealous that she is out having a fun day with her children while I am worrying about crazy things that might mean my family never gets to be the same again.

After walking through the indoor shopping centre that houses the food court and passing hundreds of shoppers as I go, I eventually make it outside to the car park and find my vehicle, before getting in behind the wheel and starting the engine. I make a quick check on my mobile again to see if Alex has tried to get in touch with me to explain his no-show, but there is still nothing, so I put my phone down on the passenger seat and start driving.

I was planning to go home but decide that there won't be much solace to be found sitting around in an empty house until the kids finish school, so I instead turn left at the traffic lights and head in the direction of my sister's house.

I know that Sarah has phoned in sick today, so she should be in, and I also know that there is nothing wrong with her, at least not health-wise. She just needed a day to deal with what is going on, and I can't blame her. She also wanted me to phone her as soon as I had finished my 'lunch date' with Alex, but I can do better than a phone call, and it will be good to speak to her face to face. But it won't be good to tell her that my husband failed to show up, and I'm still no nearer to knowing why Alex had to steal Paul's laptop.

My journey progresses smoothly because there aren't too many cars out on the roads at this time of day, so I reach Sarah's street in less than ten minutes and come to a stop outside her house. I see her car is on the drive, as it should be if she is pretending to her boss that she is 'ill' today, and I get out of my vehicle and head down the driveway towards her front door looking forward to seeing my sibling.

But my first knock on the door goes unanswered, as does my second and third one, and I'm not sure why Sarah is not coming to let me in. I try giving her mobile a ring in case she has gone out for a walk nearby, but there is no answer, and all I can think of is that she is in the shower and has failed to hear me knocking. But that's not a problem because I know where Sarah keeps the spare key, so I can just let myself in and wait for her, as I have done many times here before.

I scoop the key out from under the third plant pot on the left-hand side of the front garden and slot it into the lock before turning it and entering my sister's house.

'Hey, Sarah! It's only me! Are you in?'

I get no response from my sibling as I close the front door and take off my shoes, nor can I hear the shower running upstairs. I guess she has gone for a walk, so I hope she won't be long as I make my way into the living room to take a seat on her comfy sofa and wait.

But I freeze in the doorway, and then a scream escapes my lips when I see what is waiting for me in here.

My sister.

Lying on the carpet beside the coffee table. Eyes wide open. Body not moving.

Dead.

40

ELLEN

It's been twenty-four hours since I found my sister's body, and the shock of the traumatic event still hasn't worn off. I haven't slept since, nor have I eaten anything, and I've barely even spoken. All I can do is sit and stare into space, my face a blank canvas, devoid of emotion, and my mind failing to help me function properly as I think about how and why this has happened.

The police haven't been able to shed any light on the horrible situation yet, telling me that they are investigating it, but then they have to say that, don't they? It's their job to find out why a woman died in her own home, and they have mentioned an accident, suicide, heart attack or any number of possible reasons because they don't want to commit to anything yet, but that's only because they don't want to alarm the public by having them think there's a killer on the loose. But this was no accident, and it sure as hell wasn't suicide because my sister was not depressed. Yes, she had lost her long-term boyfriend recently, and it had been a huge shock, but she wouldn't do such a thing as take her own life. She still had family and friends, and besides, Sarah had found out that Paul was far from perfect after his death, so I know that she wasn't missing him half as much as an outside observer might think.

My sister was killed.

The question is *by whom?*

Perhaps the main reason for my lack of communication with anybody since I found my sister unresponsive on her living room floor is because I am afraid of who I think the killer might be.

My husband. The father of my two girls. The man I already know is capable of breaking into my sister's home and stealing from her.

Alex.

Murder is a big step up from burglary, but he had the motive. He had a secret, and it was one that both my sister and I were looking to bring to light. I was supposed to meet Alex at lunchtime yesterday to find out everything, but he failed to show. But did Sarah already know his truth? Is that why she is now gone? And does this explain why Alex failed to show up at the food court yesterday?

Was he at my sister's house instead, taking her life and protecting himself from whatever it was that she knew about him?

I should tell the police of my suspicions. I should tell them that I'm worried that my husband had something to do with my sister's death. I should tell them that we knew Alex had been acting strangely recently and, for some reason, knew Paul had information about Charlotte Graham on his laptop.

So why haven't I?

Because I'm scared.

I'm scared of my husband and what he might be capable of. I'm scared for myself, but most of all, I'm scared for my two girls. I can't do anything that would risk them coming to harm, and I don't know what will happen if I report Alex to the police as a potential suspect in Sarah's death. What if it was him, but there's no evidence? He'll get out of custody, and when he does, I imagine he will be very angry with me. If he can kill once, what's to stop him doing it again?

The more I think about it, the more I believe my husband is behind my sister's death.

But I'm too scared to do anything about it.

Yet, anyway.

'We need to start thinking about the funeral arrangements,' Alex says to me a few moments later when he has walked into the kitchen and seen me sitting at the table, staring at the wall with an untouched cup of coffee in front of me.

It's the cup of coffee he made me an hour ago because he said it would make me feel better, but I haven't even tried it, and now it's stone cold. Of course it wouldn't make me feel better. It won't bring back Sarah, will it? But I didn't say that at the time as he boiled the kettle and took the coffee jar from the cupboard, and I don't say anything now that he has just brought up the subject of the funeral. I know that he is right, and we do need to start thinking about the arrangements for Sarah's burial, but right now, I can barely keep myself upright in this chair, never mind start making phone calls to local funeral parlours to discuss what colour flowers she might want on her coffin.

'There won't be a funeral for a while,' I tell Alex as he picks up my wasted cup of coffee and goes to make me a new one. 'The police are still investigating, and they need her body for that.'

I glance at my husband as he fills the kettle from the tap to see if he shows any emotion at what I have just said that might give away what he thinks about the police investigation. But he remains stoic as he works, and I don't learn anything about what might be going on behind his calm mask.

'Make sure you drink this one,' he says to me a few moments later when he has made me a second coffee and placed the cup down on the table in front of me.

I nod my head to let him know that I will, but it's only so he will leave the room and leave me alone. I don't want to be around him right now. I need time to think.

I need time to figure out what I should do next.

Go to the police?

Or bury my sister and keep whatever Alex is hiding from me buried too?

41

ELLEN

Nobody ever says that it's a nice day for a funeral. People say that about weddings and birthdays but not funerals. That's because there is no such thing as a nice day to bury a loved one. It's always a bad day, even if the clouds part and the sun comes out. The sky is blue now, and the grounds of the church are bathed in brilliant sunlight, but nobody is smiling and feeling good about the world today. We're all here to pay our respects to Sarah, my wonderful sister, and the woman who the local police force have now concluded was definitely murdered in her own home.

So far, they have no suspects, but that's only because I still haven't given them one. I haven't breathed a word about my worries about Alex to anybody, and that is why he is walking beside me now with his hand in mine, telling me to stay strong as we make our way into the church where the service is due to begin shortly. Molly and Bethany are walking behind us, holding each other's hands and looking pretty but devastated in their little black dresses. I'm wearing all black too, as is every other mourner making their way inside, and no amount of sunlight can brighten up our moods today.

We stop once we reach the doorway, and then Alex reminds me that it will be nice if I was to greet some of the people who have come here today to say goodbye to Sarah. I know he is right, so I nod my head before watching him take our girls inside to find their seats. I remain by the door, standing opposite the kindly old man who will conduct today's service, and we stay standing there as more and more people arrive, passing us in the doorway and telling me how sorry they are for my loss.

It's lovely to see so many people here today coming out for Sarah, from old family members to her friends and work colleagues, but there is only one person I want to see, and it is my darling sister, standing beside me and smiling at me. It breaks my heart that we will never have another conversation again or share a bottle of wine and stay up late telling silly stories and making each other laugh with our bad jokes. It also breaks my heart that Molly and Bethany have been robbed of the perfect auntie, one who would have continued to spoil them rotten as they got older before eventually becoming a great friend of theirs when they reached adulthood. I just want Sarah back, but that is never going to happen, and today is just one more damning reminder of that fact.

It takes a while, but eventually, all the mourners are inside the church, and I make my way to the vacant space beside Alex, who is already in his seat and doing his best to keep our daughters from being too upset about things. I try not to spend too much time looking at the coffin as the service begins, but it's not easy because the wooden box is right in front of me, only a few yards away, and I know my dear sister is lying inside it. I notice that Molly and Bethany keep looking at it too, and my heart aches for my poor little girls, who are having to go through a traumatic event like this one at such an early stage in their lives. But then I look at Alex, and I see that he isn't looking at the coffin. He is staring down at the floor in front of him and doing his best not to look up.

Is it because he is upset?

Or is it because he is guilty?

I haven't dared bring up anything to do with Paul, or the laptop, or Charlotte since Sarah died, far too afraid of what Alex might end up telling me if I do. But this is no life for me now. I'm a woman in fear, and it's fear of the man I am married to. I know he is guilty of something, I'm just not exactly sure what, but my imagination likes to remind me that it could be something I'm better off not knowing. I try to keep thinking of the girls and how at the moment, they have a stable family unit. One mum. One dad. Just how it should be. Things will stay like that as long as I don't do anything to threaten it because I know Alex won't. He just wants to get on with our lives, and he wants me to do the same. The less said about the past, the better. That might not be what is best for me, but it might be what is best for the kids. Let them grow up thinking they have a perfect family. Let them enjoy their childhood. Let them develop into fully functioning adults. Maybe when that has happened, and they have moved out of home, I can see how I feel about Alex. If I want to leave him then, I can do. It will be easier to divorce when the girls are older. I don't even have to say why, just that time has passed, and my feelings are no longer the same for the man I married when I was young. If I do anything now then Alex will know it has something to do with Sarah, and Paul, and the laptop, and Charlotte. But if I wait several years, then he might not know, and he might not even care by then either.

It's going to be tough, but what else can I do? Go to the police, tell them I think my husband killed my sister and then also say that he might have had something to do with the disappearance of Charlotte Graham? If I do that then we will become the most famous family in Britain, and there will be photos of all four of us in the newspapers and on the news bulletins. I will be a single mother to two girls who will be traumatised forever and never get over both what their father did and the fact that it was their mother who got him caught. And Alex will hate me, and that is not a good thing if he is as dangerous a man as I fear he might be.

I feel trapped, just like Sarah is trapped in that box in front of me.

But I've been so preoccupied with my thoughts that I have failed to notice that the service has stopped, and everybody in attendance has turned to look back at the entrance to this church. By the time that I do, I turn around and see several police officers marching into the church, and they are all coming straight towards me.

'Mummy, what's happening?' Bethany asks me as the officers get closer to the front, but I have no answer for my daughter because I don't know.

It only takes a couple more seconds before the police officers are standing right in front of me and my family, and I'm just about to ask them what is going on when two of them reach forward and pull my husband out of his seat.

'Alex Reynolds. You are under arrest for the murder of Sarah Meadows. You do not have to say anything, but it may harm your defence if you do not mention when questioned something that you later rely on in court. Anything that you do say may be given in evidence.'

Alex is quickly handcuffed and pushed in the direction of the door, protesting his innocence as he goes, but I just stand and watch him being taken away. Molly and Bethany are crying and pulling at my hands and demanding to know what is happening to their daddy, but I don't have any words for them at this time.

I'm just watching Alex go.

And just before he leaves the church and goes to where the police car is waiting for him, he glances back at me.

And that's when I see the truth written all over his face.

EPILOGUE

ELLEN

Lies.

Everybody has told one or two in their time, and I'm no different. But that doesn't make me a bad person because the things I lied about were never going to hurt somebody else. That's the thing with lies. There are different kinds, and some are much worse than others. The lies I have told were harmless. But the lies Alex and Paul told were devastating.

I'm back at the church where my sister's funeral took place last month, but this time, I am here alone. There are no other mourners around me, nor are my daughters following behind. And my husband is certainly not holding my hand anymore. I'm by myself, and I'm here to visit Sarah's grave, where I will lay down a fresh bouquet of flowers and take a few quiet moments to think about the times we shared together, before walking away and getting on with my difficult life.

Unlike the day of the funeral, the sky is grey and the air is cold, and as I make my way through the rows of headstones, I pull my coat a little tighter around my chest. Visiting my sister's grave has always proven to be a difficult pilgrimage ever since I started making it twice a week, but it feels even harder today with this grim weather, and after the developments of yesterday when I learnt even more about what it was my husband had really been up to in secret.

There was much chaos and confusion when Alex was arrested at the funeral, and even though I had harboured my suspicions beforehand, there was still a lot for me to learn once he was in custody, and the first thing had been how he had come to be there. I hadn't reported Alex, and Sarah obviously hadn't done it from beyond the grave, so why was he arrested?

It turned out that just like so many other parts of this sorry story, a laptop held the key to the truth.

But this wasn't Paul's laptop this time. Instead, it was the laptop that my sister had borrowed from a young computer shop worker called Calvin before her untimely death. Sarah was using the laptop so that she could watch Alex using Paul's device thanks to the spyware software that had been installed, but it turned out that Calvin had installed his own secret spyware too.

It seems Calvin had quite the crush on my sister, and that was what had led him to install an application on the laptop she had borrowed in which he could see her through the camera whenever she was using it. Obviously, doing such a thing is very creepy and very stalkerish, but it turns out that in this case, the unethical behaviour of the teenager ended up solving the mystery of my sister's death. That's because Sarah had been using the laptop just before she died, and because of that fact, the camera had captured the moment when her attacker had taken her life in her living room. Calvin had seen it all happen after watching the recorded footage on his own computer at home, and while it had taken him a while to pluck up the courage to go to the police because he knew he would be in trouble for spying on Sarah in the first place, in the end, he did the right thing and handed the evidence in. That footage was brutal and raw, but it was exactly what the police needed to arrest my sister's killer. Alex had killed her, and he had been caught, and that was why he was dragged away from me and my daughters on the day of the funeral.

Faced with such damning evidence, my husband had little choice but to accept that he was going to go to prison for a very long time, so he might as well explain his actions. He had been reluctant to do so for a while, until I finally relented and agreed to pay him a visit while he was in custody. That had been the first time I had gone to see him since he had been arrested, and I had rather been hoping that I would never have to see him again once the evidence of what he had done to Sarah had been relayed to me. But my husband had been continually asking to see me, and I ultimately agreed but only with one condition.

He had to tell the truth about Paul and whatever happened with Charlotte because if not, he would never see me or his daughters again.

I found out yesterday that Alex had done the right thing and told the police the truth, and it was a truth that was shocking and devastating to learn. Paul had hit Charlotte with his car while Alex was in the passenger seat, and they had panicked before burying her body in the woods. Paul had felt guilty and kept photos on his laptop, which could have given away his guilt, so Alex had contrived to delete that evidence after his friend's death. Sarah had discovered this, and Alex had ultimately confessed to her what he had done with

Charlotte in the hope that she would keep it secret for the sake of her sister's family life. But then Alex had apparently realised that he couldn't trust Sarah to stay quiet, and that was why he had gone to her house when he was supposed to be meeting me for lunch and killed her, unwittingly in full view of the laptop camera on which Calvin was secretly recording. Alex had then told the police the location of Charlotte's body, and sure enough, the investigating officers had been able to find it and provide some much needed closure for the young student's disconsolate family.

It could never make up for what Alex and Paul did, but at least there was no more mystery to torment the poor woman's family for the rest of their days. And there was no more mystery for me either after that. I now know exactly what kind of man my husband is and what he is capable of. He buried a woman, he tried to cover it up, and when it was exposed, he panicked and killed my sister. He deserves to rot in a prison cell for the rest of his life, and he almost certainly will. But I don't deserve what is happening, my daughters don't deserve it, and Sarah certainly didn't deserve this either.

I stop walking when I reach her gravestone, and I crouch down to place the fresh flowers in front of the inscribed words that let everybody who visits this site know exactly who this deceased person was and what they meant to so many.

Standing back up, I take a moment to read the epitaph, even though I've already read it dozens of times since I've been coming here and leaving flowers in my sister's memory.

SARAH MEADOWS 1985 – 2021

BELOVED DAUGHTER, SISTER, AUNTIE & FRIEND.

TAKEN FAR TOO SOON BUT CHERISHED FOREVER BY ALL THOSE WHO KNEW HER.

REST IN PEACE

I wipe a tear from my left eye as I finish reading the inscription before taking a quiet moment to reflect on one of my fondest memories of my sister, which came when we were youngsters holidaying with our parents in Cornwall. I was six, and Sarah was eight, and we were on our way back to the hotel after a day at the beach, when we stopped to get ice creams. I ordered two scoops of chocolate while Sarah got her usual vanilla flavour, and then we set off in the direction of mum and dad's car. But we had barely taken a couple of steps before I tripped and sent my ice cream cone flying through the air before it came to a very sloppy halt on the concrete floor in front of me. Needless to say, as a young child, I had been devastated at what had happened and had turned back to my parents to beg for them to buy me a replacement ice cream. But they had told me that they had no more spare change so they wouldn't be able to do that for me. That was terrible news, and I had been on the verge of having a tantrum when Sarah very kindly and very surprisingly offered me her ice cream instead. It wasn't chocolate, but it was better than nothing, and it had been enough to make me feel better and stop the tears from flowing.

I had only been young then, but I always remembered that time and not least of all because Sarah would remind me of it over the years as we grew up. She would always say, 'Remember when I gave you my ice cream?' if we were arguing or often even in the good times, and I guess it was her way of reminding me how much she loved me. It was that kind gesture that made me so keen to see my daughters share things with each other because it's not the sharing that counts so much as it is the meaning behind it. People who love each other share, and after that day when I was six years old, I was never in any doubt that my sister loved me ever again.

I re-read her epitaph one more time before turning and walking away, making my way back through the graveyard in the direction of my parked car. But as I go, I pass another gravestone here that is familiar to me, and I pause to read the first part of this epitaph too.

PAUL BARBER 1985 – 2021

But I stop before reading anymore because it doesn't matter what it says about him being a beloved son, boyfriend or friend. The only thing that would matter is if it said the truth, which it never will because the truth is not always the thing that ends up on somebody's gravestone.

If this inscription was honest then it would say the same thing that should go on Alex's gravestone when he eventually dies one day. It's a succinct engraving, and it wouldn't take somebody long to make it at all.

It's just four words. A simple sentence.

But it would sum up both Paul and Alex very well.

HE WAS A LIAR.

Download My Free Book

If you would like to receive a FREE copy of my psychological thriller 'Just One Second' then you can find the link to the book at my website www.danielhurstbooks.com

LETTER FROM THE AUTHOR

Thank you for reading *He Was A Liar* and I hope you had as much fun delving into the lives of Sarah, Paul, Ellen and Alex as I had creating them. I love to write, and I hope my story gave you a little entertainment and escapism from the realities of the world.

Without readers like you, I wouldn't be living my dream as a full-time author, so thank you for picking up this book and thank you for any review you may choose to leave for it afterwards. Reviews really are the most powerful way of getting attention for my books as they help bring in new readers. If you have enjoyed this book then I would be extremely grateful if you could spend a couple of minutes leaving an honest review on Amazon or Goodreads (it can be as short as you like).

Thank you and I hope you enjoy your next read.

Daniel

Also By Daniel Hurst

TIL DEATH DO US PART

What if your husband was your worst enemy?

Megan thinks that she has the perfect husband and the perfect life. Craig works all day so that she doesn't have to, leaving her free to relax in their beautiful and secluded country home. But when she starts to long for friends and purpose again, Megan applies for a job in London, much to her husband's disappointment. She thinks he is upset because she is unhappy. But she has no idea.

When Megan secretly attends an interview and meets a recruiter for a drink, Craig decides it is time to act. Locking her away in their home, Megan realises that her husband never had her best interests at heart. Worse, they didn't meet by accident. Craig has been planning it all from the start.

As Megan is kept shut away from the world with only somebody else's diary for company, she starts to uncover the lies, the secrets, and the fact that she isn't actually Craig's first wife after all...

OUT NOW

THE WOMAN AT THE DOOR

It was a perfect Saturday night. ***Until she knocked on the door...***

Rebecca and Sam are happily married and enjoying a typical Saturday night until a knock at the door changes everything. There's a woman outside, and she has something to say. Something that will change the happy couple's relationship forever...

With their marriage thrown into turmoil, Rebecca no longer knows who to trust, while Sam is determined to find out who that woman was and why she came to their house. But the problem is that he doesn't know who she is and why she has targeted them.

Desperate to save his marriage, Sam is willing to do anything to find the truth, even if it means breaking the law. But as time goes by and things only seem to get worse, it looks like he could lose Rebecca forever.

Nobody knows the woman at the door. ***But she knows you.***

THE NEIGHBOURS

It seemed like the perfect house on the perfect street.
Until they met the neighbours...

Happily married couple Katie and Sean have plenty to look forward to as they move into their new home and plan for the future. But then they meet two of their new neighbours and everything on their quiet street suddenly doesn't seem as desirable as it did before.

Having been warned about the other neighbours, and their adulterous and criminal ways, Katie and Sean realise that they are going to have to be on their guard if they want to make their time here a happy one.

But some of the other neighbours seem so nice and that's why they choose to ignore the warning and get friendly with the rest of the people on the street. *And that is why their marriage will never be the same again...*

Four houses. Six neighbours. ***And one shocking twist.***

THE TUTOR

What if you invited danger into your home?

Amy is a loving wife and mother, to her husband Nick, and her two children, Michael and Bella. It's that dedication to her family that causes her to seek help for her teenage son when it becomes apparent that he is going to fail his end of school exams.

Enlisting the help of a professional tutor, Amy is certain that she is doing the best thing for her son, and indeed, her family. But when she discovers that there is more to this tutor than meets the eye, it is already too late.

With the rest of her family enamoured by the tutor, Amy is the only one who can see that there is something not quite right about her. But as the tutor becomes more involved in Amy's family, it's not just the present that is threatened. Secrets from the past are exposed too, and by the time everything is out in the open, Amy isn't just worried about her son and his exams anymore. She is worried for the survival of her entire family.

This will be one lesson they will never forget.

OUT NOW

RUN AWAY WITH ME

What if your partner was wanted by the police?

Laura is feeling content with her life. She is married, she has a good home, and she is due to give birth to her first child any day now. But her perfect world is shattered when her husband comes home flustered and afraid. He's made a terrible mistake. He's done a bad thing. *And now the police are going to be looking for him.*

There's only one way out of this. He wants to run. *But he won't go without his wife…*

Laura knows it is wrong. She knows they should stay and face the music. But she doesn't want to lose her man. She can't raise this baby alone. *So she agrees to go with him.* But life on the run is stressful and unpredictable and as time goes by, Laura worries she has made a terrible mistake. They should never have ran. But it's too late for that now. Her life is ruined. The only question is: *how will it end?*

OUT NOW

THE ROLE MODEL

She raised her. Now she must help her…

Heather is a single mum who has always done what's best for her daughter, Chloe. From childhood up to the age of seventeen, Chloe has been no trouble. That is until one night when she calls her mother with some shocking news.

There's been an accident. *And now there's a dead body…*

As always, Heather puts her daughter's safety before all else, but this might be one time when she goes too far. Instead of calling the emergency services, Heather hides the body, saving her daughter from police interviews and public outcry.

But as she well knows, everything she does has an impact on her child's behaviour, and as time goes on and the pair struggle to keep their sordid secret hidden, Heather begins to think that she hasn't been such a good mum after all.

In fact, she might have been the worst role model ever…

OUT NOW

THE BROKEN VOWS

He broke his word to her. Now she wants revenge...

Alison is happily married to Graham, or at least she is until she finds out that he has been cheating on her. Graham has broken the vows he made on his wedding day. How could he do it? It takes Alison a while to figure it out, but at least she has time on her side. *Only that is where she is wrong.*

A devastating diagnosis means the clock is ticking down on her life now and if she wants revenge on her cheating partner then she is going to have to act fast. Alison does just that, implementing a dangerous and deadly plan, and it's one that will have far reaching consequences for several people, including her clueless husband.

Hell hath no fury like a woman scorned...

OUT NOW

INFLUENCE

Would you kill for a million followers?

Emily Bennett dreams of being a social media influencer, just like her idols, Mason Manor & Ivy Lane. But shortly after Ivy's untimely death she is contacted by a secretive businessman who offers her the chance at the fame and fortune she so desperately craves.

While Emily initially gets to experience the things she has always wanted, it soon becomes clear that her new employer had sinister motives for approaching her and it isn't long before she discovers that the life of her dreams comes with the kind of conditions that are the stuff of nightmares.

Social media isn't life or death.

It's more important than that.

OUT NOW

THE 20 MINUTE SERIES

20 Chapters. 20 Characters. 20 intertwining stories.

An original psychological thriller series showing how we are all more connected to each other than we think.

What readers are saying:

"If you like people watching then you will love these books!"

"The psychological insight was fascinating, the stories were absorbing and the characters were 3D. I absolutely loved it."

"The books in this series are an incredibly easy read, you become invested in the lives of the characters so easily and I am eager to know more and more. Roll on the next book."

THE 20 MINUTES SERIES (in order)

20 MINUTES ON THE TUBE
20 MINUTES LATER
20 MINUTES IN THE PARK
20 MINUTES ON HOLIDAY
20 MINUTES BY THE THAMES
20 MINUTES AT HALLOWEEN
20 MINUTES AROUND THE BONFIRE
20 MINUTES BEFORE CHRISTMAS
20 MINUTES OF VALENTINE'S DAY
20 MINUTES TO CHANGE A LIFE
20 MINUTES IN LAS VEGAS
20 MINUTES IN THE DESERT
20 MINUTES ON THE ROAD
20 MINUTES BEFORE THE WEDDING

About The Author

Daniel Hurst lives in the North West of England with his wife, Harriet, and considers himself extremely fortunate to be able to write stories every day for his readers.

You can visit him at his online home www.danielhurstbooks.com

You can connect with Daniel on Facebook at www.facebook.com/danielhurstbooks or on Instagram at www.instagram.com/danielhurstbooks

He is always happy to receive emails from readers at daniel@danielhurstbooks.com and replies to every single one.

Thank you for reading.

Daniel

Made in United States
North Haven, CT
12 May 2022

19111829R00162